Angela Somme

the little Vampire
IN DANGER

Illustrated by Amelie Glienke

Translated by Sarah Gibson

SIMON & SCHUSTER

LONDON • SYDNEY • NEW YORK • TOKYO • SINGAPORE • TORONTO

Copyright © 1985 Rowohlt Taschenbuch Verlag GmbH

First published in Germany in 1985 by
Rowohlt Taschenbuch Verlag GmbH

First published in Great Britain in 1991
by Simon and Schuster Young Books

Photoset in North Wales by
Derek Doyle & Associates, Mold, Clwyd.
Printed and bound in Great Britain by
The Guernsey Press Co. Ltd, Guernsey, Channel Islands.

Simon and Schuster Young Books
Simon and Schuster Ltd
Wolsey House
Wolsey Road
Hemel Hempstead HP2 4SS

British Library Cataloguing in Publication Data
Sommer-Bodenburg, Angela
  Little vampire in danger, the.
  I. Title   II. Series
  823'.914 [J]

ISBN 0 7500 0407 X
ISBN 0 7500 0408 8 (Pbk)

Contents

The Photograph 1
Tapping Signals from the Other World 5
Thirst 10
Eavesdroppers on the Balcony 14
Voices of the Night 21
Visiting the Invalid 25
The Emergency Exit 31
A New Excuse 34
The Prescription 37
Tulli-Ex 43
An Unexpected Meeting 46
Being Clean 52
Something Terrible is Going to Happen! 56
Don't Get Your Knickers in a Twist! 59
More Difficulties 63
The Wreckers of the Environment 65
Boys Will Be Boys 69
A Real Nature Conservationist 72
Revenge on the Brain 77
A Visit to the Psychologist 83
The Most Important Person 87
Ice-Cream and Red Ears 92
Beating Hearts 97
A Symphony in Horror 102
The Last Time 105
The Frog Prince 108
The Cute Blond One 114
The Pledge 118

*for Katja, who is
also extremely brave,*

This book is for Burghardt,
who looks danger in the face

*and for everyone who is daring enough
to read vampire stories.*

The Characters
in this Book

Tony is a boy who loves reading
horror stories.
His favourite books are
about vampires, and he
knows all about
their habits and the
way they live.

Tony's parents don't really believe
in vampires.

Tony's father works in an office; his mother is a teacher.

Rudolph, the Little Vampire, has
been a vampire for at least
a hundred and fifty years.
He became a vampire
while he was still
a child and that is
why he is so small. His

friendship with Tony began when Tony was all alone in his house yet again. Suddenly, there was the Little Vampire sitting on the windowsill. Tony was terrified, but the Little Vampire reassured him that he had already "eaten". In fact, Tony had imagined vampires would be much more frightening, and after Rudolph had told him how much he, too, loved reading vampire stories, and admitted that he was afraid of the dark, Tony began to get on well with him. From that moment on, Tony's rather boring life became very exciting. The Little Vampire brought him a special cloak, and together they flew to the cemetery and to the Sackville-Bagg family vault. Soon Tony had got to know other members of the vampire family:

Anna is Rudolph's sister –
his "little" sister, as he
likes to point out.
In fact, Anna is nearly
as strong as Rudolph,
and much braver than he.
She likes vampire stories, too.

Gruesome Gregory, Rudolph's elder brother,
is a very irritable vampire.
His croaky voice goes up
and down, which shows he
is still an adolescent.
The worst of it is
he will never grow out
of this difficult phase
because he became a
vampire during puberty.

Aunt Dorothy is the most blood-thirsty vampire of them all. Your life would certainly be in danger if you bumped into her after dark.

Tony has not met the Little Vampire's other relations personally, but he has seen their coffins in the family vault.

The night-watchman of the cemetery, Mr McRookery, is always hunting vampires. That is why the vampires have moved their coffins to an underground vault. McRookery has not yet managed to find the entrance to the vault.

Sniveller comes from Watford and is the assistant gardener. His job is to help McRookery keep the cemetery tidy and to hunt down the vampires.

The Photograph

When Tony appeared at breakfast on that Saturday morning, he sensed immediately that something unpleasant was in the air. At first sight, everything seemed normal: there were fresh bread rolls on the table, music was coming from the radio, and yet . . .

He sat down, began to spread butter on his roll, and waited. He did not have to wait for long.

His father cleared his throat and said, "Tony, we've got to talk to you."

"Talk to me?" said Tony, and he tried to pour himself some milk in a deliberately casual way. Needless to say, his hand shook, and he spilled half of it on the tablecloth.

"Can't you be more careful?" his mother exclaimed in annoyance.

Tony fetched a cloth.

"Now then . . ." Dad began again. "It's about those strange friends of yours."

"Which friends?" Tony pretended not to understand.

"Anna and Rudolph."

Tony felt his cheeks growing red. It always happened when the conversation got on to the subject of his best friends: the Little Vampire, Rudolph Sackville-Bagg, and his sister, Anna.

1

"What about them?"

"Here!" Dad pulled a long red envelope from the inside pocket of his jacket. It was an envelope of newly developed photographs.

"So what?" Tony shrugged his shoulders. He was not interested in his parents' snapshots, for goodness sake!

"Just have a look at them!" said Mum coldly.

"If you like . . ." Tony took the pile of photographs out of the envelope and reluctantly began to look through them. The first few were exactly what he had expected: boring snapshots of houses, trees, clouds . . .

But then! Tony gave a start.

It was the picture that Dad had taken the previous Saturday of Tony and Anna. Tony recognized the scraps of paper on the carpet, the pots of flowers toppled on the floor, the rumpled sofa cushions . . . but there was no sign of Anna. She was not in the photograph, although she had been standing next to Tony when his father took it.

He could still remember vividly how the blinding flash had frightened her, and how she had covered her face with her hands with a cry.

He was still looking at the photo in disbelief when he heard his father say, "There you are! And now I'd like to hear what you have to say about it."

"About what?" asked Tony.

"I know perfectly well," Dad answered in some annoyance, "that I took a photo of both of you. So why isn't Anna in the picture?"

"Why ask me?" Tony stammered.

"Because they're your friends," Mum exclaimed, "these – vampires!"

It was the first time that she had not said "vampires" in a scornful, jeering way. Now the word suddenly sounded serious and menacing – as if she believed in vampires herself.

Tony was much too confused to think of a good reply. He knew that vampires have no reflection – but he had had no idea that you could not capture their image in a photograph either.

"I . . . I expect you didn't get her properly in the picture," he mumbled.

"Not in the picture!" his father retorted crossly. "Take another look at the photo!"

Tony did – and there he saw something totally and absolutely unbelievable: there was a book apparently floating in mid-air. He turned the photograph round so he could read the title. It was *Romeo and Juliet*, the book that Anna had been reading on Saturday. It was floating in the exact place where Anna's hand must have been: but Anna's hand was not there.

Incredible . . . but Tony had the proof before his very eyes! He noticed that his parents were watching him. He would have to say something – but what could he say?

"The book –" he began. "It looks as if it's just falling to the ground."

"No." His mother shook her head vigorously. "It looks as if someone is holding it."

Tony quickly picked up his mug of milk, to hide just how shaken he was. As calmly as he could, he said, "But how could it be? The person would have to be invisible."

"Or a vampire!" his mother added, watching him keenly. "Vampires don't have a reflection, do they?"

"You could be right."

"And if you don't have a reflection, you wouldn't show up in a photograph, would you?"

"I thought you didn't believe in vampires!" Tony remarked.

"Up till now I didn't. But now I've seen that photo . . ." After a pause she continued, "Tonight your father and I have been invited to Dr Dozee's. We'll be able to put the whole matter to her."

"What 'whole matter'?" asked Tony uneasily.

"Your links with these –" she hesitated, and tried to find the right expression, "with these – apparitions!"

A cold shiver ran through Tony. It seemed things were becoming steadily more and more risky – for himself, for the Little Vampire, and for Anna.

So he objected cautiously, "But why? What's Dr Dozee got to do with it?"

"You just leave that to us!" his mother countered coolly.

Dad agreed. "We'll see what we'll see tomorrow morning."

Tony pressed his lips together and was silent. What else could he do?

He could only wait and hope: wait to see what Dr Dozee would say, and hope that the Little Vampire would come to see him that evening.

Tapping Signals from the Other World

After his parents had left, Tony waited at the open window. A chilly wind was blowing, and he folded his arms with a shiver. He wouldn't be able to stand here for long . . .

It was just after eight o'clock, and there were lights in the windows of many of the flats. At this time of day most people were sitting in front of the television. It was a convenient time for Rudolph to fly around without being seen.

Tony strained his eyes, but he couldn't see the Little Vampire anywhere. By now he was getting so cold he was trembling. He went to his cupboard and pulled on a thick jumper.

When he came back, he caught sight of a shadow in the outside corner of the window, and then came the sound of muffled laughter. There was only one person who laughed like that!

"Rudolph!" said Tony in delight.

"Good evening, Tony," the Little Vampire greeted him, and climbed into the room. He glanced at the door and asked suspiciously, "Are your parents here?"

"No. They've gone out."

"To the cinema?"

"No."

"To the theatre?"

Tony shook his head.

"Aha – they've gone dancing then!" the vampire announced, grinning knowingly.

"I wish they had," Tony answered gloomily.

"Why, where are they?" The Little Vampire was suddenly all ears.

Tony sighed. "They're with Dr Dozee. To discuss vampires."

"What?" the Little Vampire yelped.

"Yes. It's all that stupid photo's fault."

"What photo?"

"The one Dad took last Saturday of Anna and me. Anna doesn't show up in the photo, but the book she was holding does."

"Bother! She must have realized that would happen," said the vampire, whistling softly through his teeth. "Our parents have taught us never to let ourselves be photographed."

"Anna didn't want to be." Tony was quick to defend her. "But Dad just pressed the button."

"Did he use a flash?"

Tony nodded.

"Oh, dear!" said the vampire and began to pace slowly up and down the room. His face looked strained and anxious. "Now I see where Anna's got her mysterious illness from."

"Is Anna not well?" Tony asked in dismay.

The vampire threw him a gloomy look. "She's been lying in her coffin for a whole week. She's got a terrible headache and if she stands up, she gets all dizzy. And she can't see properly – everything looks blurred."

Tony was upset, and he clapped a hand to his mouth.

It was his fault that Anna wasn't well – just because she had wanted to stay with him last Saturday evening when his parents came back unexpectedly.

"Can't someone help her?" he asked.

The vampire shrugged his shoulders helplessly. "How?"

There was a pause.

Then Tony asked, "Did you bring the second cloak with you?"

The vampire nodded and pulled out a tattered vampire cloak from under his own.

"Here. I thought we could do something together."

"No thanks," said Tony. "I'd rather go and see Anna. Perhaps I can do something for her."

"You?" said the vampire, looking at Tony's neck with a grin. Slowly he drew the tip of his tongue over his

7

pointed canine teeth. "Yes, well, perhaps. Why not . . . ?"

Tony hastily turned up the collar of his jumper. "I wasn't thinking of that," he said. "Anyway, Anna still drinks milk, doesn't she?"

"Only in emergencies," the vampire answered roughly.

"Well, this is an emergency," Tony declared. He stood up and went to the kitchen.

In the fridge he found two cartons of milk, one opened and the other still sealed. Tony took the latter, put it in a plastic bag and went back to Rudolph.

The vampire was sitting on Tony's bed, leafing through a book. It was *Tapping Signals from the Other World*, which Tony had bought just a couple of days earlier and was reading every night before he went to sleep.

"Is it good? Can I take it with me for a while?" asked Rudolph, already beginning to tuck the book away under his cloak.

From past experience, Tony knew that he was most unlikely ever to get the book back again. So he said in a rather bored voice, "Exciting? No, it's slow and rather dull."

"Slow? Dull?" the vampire barked, flinging the book away from him in disgust. It bounced against the cupboard and fell on the carpet. "Boring books should be banned!"

"Yeah," Tony muttered, bending down quickly to pick up the book before the vampire could see how pleased he was.

"So why do you read books like that?" the vampire enquired.

"Why?" Tony repeated.

Luckily the book had only got a slight dent in it. He put it back on the shelf with deliberate care, giving him time to think up an answer.

"Because it's good for my education," he said at last, and continued in the sort of voice a head teacher would use. "Not all the books you read should be exciting ones."

"Education – pooh!" the vampire snapped scornfully. He leapt up from the bed and began to shake his scraggy arms and legs, as if they had gone to sleep. "Shall we fly, at last?" he growled.

"If you like," said Tony, slipping on the vampire cloak.

"What about that bag?" the vampire asked, nodding his head towards the plastic carrier.

"There's milk in it. For Anna."

"And how are you going to fly with that?"

"Fly?" Tony hadn't thought of that.

"Now, you see, what would you do without me?" said the vampire more gently. "If it weren't for me, you would have crashed to the ground."

Tony peeped down into the darkness uneasily.

"But you can give *me* the bag," Rudolph said boastfully. He grabbed it and leapt out into the night.

Tony sat on the windowsill for a moment and watched as the Little Vampire tried unsuccessfully to keep his balance. He soon had to make an emergency landing in the branches of the chestnut tree.

"So much for the expert!" Tony giggled.

He spread his arms wide and flew off.

Thirst

When Tony reached the tree, the Little Vampire was just tearing open the milk carton with his knobbly fingers.

"Hey, what are you doing?" Tony cried crossly.

"I'm thirsty," the vampire answered in a hollow voice, "and that's why I landed in this tree."

"But that milk is for Anna!"

Without taking any notice of Tony's protests, the vampire put the carton to his lips. But he only took the tiniest sip – then he threw the carton away with a loud "Eeugh!"

Tony saw it hit the grass under the tree and explode.

"That was mean!" he said furiously. "You know you don't like milk."

"Don't I?" said the vampire with an empty smile. "Then why would I have opened the carton?"

"I'll tell you why! Because you needed an excuse to throw it away. You simply won't admit that you very nearly had a crash."

Tony could tell he had hit the nail on the head with this remark. The vampire's reaction was an embarrassed grin. But he quickly controlled himself again.

"Rubbish!" he growled. "I was just thirsty, that's all."

And with a glance at Tony's neck, he added, "Or perhaps today you'd let me —"

"Of course not!" Tony answered quickly, feeling his hair stand on end under the menacing eyes of the vampire.

"Truly not?" The vampire leant forward a little. "Not even a little bite?"

"No!" Tony backed away from him. "And now stop it! After all, we are friends, aren't we?"

At that moment, they became aware of a noise at the bottom of the tree. It was the noise of scratching and the smacking of lips, and then came a woman's voice: "Susie! Where are you?"

"Mrs Starling!" Tony whispered to the Little Vampire.

Mrs Starling stood on the flagstone path, a dog-lead in her hand, searching for her dachshund.

"Susie-Lou! Come to Mummy now, there's a good dog!' Mrs Starling entreated, but Susie was not thinking about coming back. She was lapping up the spilt milk – and she was doing it so loudly that even Mrs Starling could hear her.

"Susie? Is that you under the tree?" Now her voice didn't sound quite so gentle. "Susie! A smart dog like you shouldn't mess around in the dirt like that!"

But even this did not have the slightest effect on Susie. She went on lapping unconcernedly.

"Come *here!*"

Susie lifted her head, licked her lips, and bent down over the milk once more."

"Just you wait! I'll teach you not to come when you're called!" Snorting like a steam train, Mrs Starling advanced on the tree, swinging the lead threateningly.

That worked. Susie gave a couple of barks, then ran to the bushes by the playground.

"You naughty, dirty little dog, you!" Mrs Starling cursed and lumbered off after the dachshund.

"Phew!" said the vampire when she had disappeared. "I wouldn't like to be her dog."

"That's what my parents always say," Tony giggled.

"Your parents —" The Vampire suddenly seemed to have thought of something important. "Didn't you say they'd gone to talk about vampires to a Dr – what's she called – Dreamer?"

"Dr Dozee," Tony corrected.

"Who is she?"

"Our GP."

"And why exactly do they want to talk about vampires?"

"Because that stupid photo has made them suspicious."

"Because Anna isn't in it?"

"Yeah. They didn't believe in vampires before. But now . . ."

"And does Dr Dozee believe in vampires?"

"I don't know."

"Hmm." The vampire chewed his lower lip thoughtfully. "Do you know where she lives?"

"Yes." Tony pointed to a house at the end of the estate. "Down there."

"Why don't we fly over?" the vampire suggested.

"Over there?" Tony was not keen. "I suppose you want to introduce yourself?"

"No." The vampire laughed softly. "But I do want to look through her window. Perhaps we'll be able to hear what they're talking about."

"Hey, brilliant idea!" Tony admitted. "I'd never have thought of that."

"But I did!" the vampire said with a grin.

Eavesdroppers on the Balcony

Dr Dozee's house was smaller than the other houses on the estate and it stood a little to one side. It was two storeys high: Dr Dozee had her surgery on the ground floor, and she lived in a flat above it. Tony had often been to the surgery, but never before to her home, so he could only guess which must be the living-room window: the one behind the enormous window-box. Muffled voices could be heard through the balcony door, which was slightly ajar.

"Is that your parents?" asked the vampire.

"Yes, definitely," Tony nodded.

"Great," said the vampire contentedly, and he landed on the balcony.

Tony followed him hesitantly. Luckily, there was a little niche by the side of the door to the balcony where they could hide. It was so narrow that they had to squeeze in very close to each other, which was rather unpleasant for Tony. The smell of mould coming from Rudolph practically took his breath away. His heart was in his mouth and he did not know which he was more afraid of: his parents and Dr Dozee, or the Little Vampire, who suddenly seemed much more dangerous at close quarters. Even now, Rudolph's lips were parting in a grin, showing those gleaming white, pointed teeth . . .

"Are you scared?" he asked.

"Sc-scared? Why should I be?" Tony answered defensively.

"Oh, I just thought you were. I must have made a mistake."

". . . *Sadly, this year we won't be able to take a holiday.*" It was a man's voice they could hear. Presumably it belonged to Mr Dozee.

"There's definitely something making a hammering noise nearby," the Little Vampire declared darkly. "Are you sure it isn't your heart?"

"My heart?" Tony turned red. "No. It's the vampire-detection device that Dr Dozee has had installed in her living-room."

The vampire's cocky smile vanished. "A vampire-detection device?" he asked nervously.

"Sssh!" Tony put a finger to his lips. "Not so loud, or the alarm will go off!"

"But next summer we'll definitely try to go to Tunisia," said a woman's voice. Tony recognized it as belonging to Dr Dozee. "We'll really be in need of a holiday by then."

"Morocco's nice, too." That was Tony's mother's voice.

"Much nicer than Nether Bogsbottom!" Tony grunted, remembering the ill-fated holiday they had spent on a farm.

"Don't remind me!" the Little Vampire groaned softly. The holiday in Nether Bogsbottom had nearly cost him his life.

"Next year, we'll be going to the seaside," Tony's mother continued. "Really because of Tony."

Tony pricked up his ears. Now this was beginning to sound interesting.

"Yes. Sea air is so good for you," Dr Dozee agreed. "Especially if you're the kind of person who is inclined to catch a cold."

"Actually, Tony doesn't often catch colds." It was his father's voice now. "But something else has been worrying us – mmm, how can I put it?"

He hesitated. He was probably afraid of sounding ridiculous if he began talking about vampires.

"Tony has such peculiar friends." Mum came to his rescue. "Their faces are completely white, they're always going around in long black cloaks – yes, and we've never seen any of them in daylight."

"Grrrr." The vampire gave a low growl.

Dr Dozee laughed. "They sound like typical street kids."

"I wouldn't quite say that," Tony's father put in, and cleared his throat. "We think they're – they might be vampires!"

There was a pause. Tony heard Rudolph hissing as he breathed in and out.

Then Dr Dozee said, "Vampires?" Her voice sounded rather amused. "But that's just superstitious nonsense – and out of date at that!"

"Well, we thought so, too, for a long time," said Tony's mother. "But see for yourself."

"Now she's showing her the photo," Tony whispered to the Little Vampire.

"I don't see anything wrong," said Dr Dozee.

"The book!" Tony's mother prompted her.

"Oh, yes. It seems to be floating in mid-air. Strange . . ."

"It's not floating in mid-air," said Tony's father. "A girl's holding it in her hand."

"Where's the girl?"

"Well, that's what we're wondering," said Dad. "I only know that she was standing next to Tony when I took the photo – and she had the book in her hand."

"Yes, that really is very strange . . ." Now Dr Dozee was sounding somewhat confused, Tony thought.

"But there must be some perfectly reasonable explanation." That was Mr Dozee's voice.

"Such as? Are you saying we vampires aren't reasonable?" the Little Vampire grumbled.

"Perhaps something happened when the photo was being developed?" Dr Dozee suggested.

"No," Dad replied. "We've tried that already. She doesn't appear on the negative either."

"And what has Tony got to do with all this?" Dr Dozee wanted to know.

Tony's father hesitated. "Supposing these friends of his really are vampires . . . Well, we're worried that they might have —" He didn't go on, assuming Dr Dozee would get the point. But she was obviously very slow on the uptake.

"*What* might they have done?" she asked. "I don't understand."

Tony giggled softly. "Dr Dozee isn't making it easy for them!"

"Well," Mum began. Her voice betrayed her discomfort. "We think that they may have – possibly – sucked his blood."

"Sucked his blood?" Dr Dozee repeated in disbelief. "But —" Then she laughed. "No, no, that's just too far-fetched!"

"We'd have said just that two days ago," Tony's father agreed. "But this photo has made us suspicious. Now we're wondering if we shouldn't have been much more careful earlier on."

"How do you mean?"

"Well, Tony's friends – we never liked them, even at the start."

"The feeling is entirely mutual!" the Little Vampire growled.

"And all this vampire business that Tony seems so bewitched by. We never took it seriously. Perhaps we should have given it more consideration."

"And now you really believe there are such things as vampires?"

"It's just that we're worried stiff about Tony," Mum replied evasively.

"That I can understand," said Dr Dozee. There was a pause, and then she suggested, "I could give him a blood test."

"What?" Tony cried. Immediately the Little Vampire clamped a bony hand over his mouth.

"Idiot!" he hissed.

"A blood test, yes, that's a good idea," Tony's mother agreed.

"No one's going to get any blood from me!" said Tony through clenched teeth.

"Oh no?" The vampire leered. "Not even me?"

"Hey, leave off!" Tony tried to push the vampire away.

"Don't you like me any more?" the Little Vampire asked, moving his face closer to Tony's neck.

"I'll scream!" Tony warned.

"Spoilsport!" The vampire turned away with a hurt expression on his face.

"When should we come for the blood test?" Tony's mother was asking.

"What does she mean, we?" said Tony grimly. He heard Dr Dozee's reply.

"Come on Monday at half past seven." Then she went on in a chatty tone of voice. "So, you're thinking of going to the seaside next year? Have you decided where, exactly?"

"No," said Dad. "Can you suggest somewhere?"

"Here we go, boring," the vampire groaned. "I've had enough of this. Let's fly!"

"To see Anna?" asked Tony happily.

"If it's absolutely necessary . . ."

Quietly, they climbed up on the balcony railings and, without anyone noticing, flew off into the night.

Voices of the Night

Just before they reached the old wall of the cemetery, the vampire suddenly said, "I've just changed my mind. I'm not coming with you."

"What?" Tony cried. "Are you deserting me?"

"Deserting you? You're exaggerating again," said the vampire grumpily. "I just don't want to be a gooseberry, that's all."

"But you know I've never gone into the vault by myself before," Tony called.

"Well, there's a first time for everything!" the vampire retorted, and he soared away.

"Traitor!" said Tony furiously, and landed in the long grass behind the cemetery wall.

He looked over at the tall yew tree with a shiver. Under it lay the entrance to the vault. Did he dare push the stone away and let himself slip down into the darkness?

He thought of Anna. She must be so lonely down there by herself, abandoned by all the vampires. As usual, they were only interested in looking after their own needs – just like Rudolph! Supposing Anna's headache and blurred vision had got worse?

The thought of that touched a nerve in Tony. He

wanted so badly to tell her how sorry he was. If only it wasn't quite so dangerous . . .

The cemetery was full of strange and sinister noises. Tony did not have a vampire's sharp eyes or sensitive ears, and he was not used to all the voices of the night. He heard things clicking and crackling, rustling and whispering, and he did not know where the noises were coming from. And supposing he did manage to get down into the vault safe and sound – would he be able to get out again? Not on his own, that was for sure, and Anna might be too weak to help him.

As he stood there, unable to make up his mind, he suddenly caught the sound of voices.

Tony felt as if he was turning into a block of ice. The voices could be coming from one of two possible sources: either the vampires or Mr McRookery, the night-watchman of the cemetery, and his assistant gardener, Sniveller.

His first thought was to run away. But then he told himself that it would be the quickest way for them to notice him. And if it *were* vampires, he would get caught without much difficulty.

He looked around anxiously and, to his great relief, caught sight of a fallen tree. He quickly ran over to it and crept right in between its branches. It was not a moment too soon, for now he could see two figures coming closer. His heart was beating fit to burst.

Just at that moment, the moon came out from behind a cloud and Tony could see that it was McRookery and Sniveller. They were wearing grey working clothes, and out of their pockets poked long, pointed wooden stakes.

Tony realized he had goose-pimples. Just don't move a muscle! he thought to himself, and drew the cloak over his head like a hood.

"Nothing there! We're too late again!" he heard McRookery growl hoarsely.

Sniveller lowered his wooden stake. His voice sounded relieved as he answered, "So the birds have flown again, have they?"

"And it's all because of you," McRookery grumbled. "You took so long having a bath."

"But I was very dirty," Sniveller defended himself. "I'd spent the whole day grubbing about in the black earth of the cemetery and I had to get cleaned up first."

"Pooh – cleaned up!" McRookery growled. "It's getting on my nerves, your fixation about getting cleaned up. Someone works in a cemetery and who minds a bit of dirt under his fingernails should think of changing his job."

"What did you say?" Sniveller cried, sounding shocked. "Do you mean you don't want me around any more?"

"No, no, of course not," said McRookery soothingly. "You know how much we've got to do in the next few weeks." His voice grew more enthusiastic as he added, "Very soon we'll have turned this wilderness into a beautiful garden, and then . . ." He paused before continuing more loudly. ". . . and then that will be the end of that rabble of vampires, that band of bloodsuckers, once and for all!"

"Well, yes, o-of course," Sniveller stuttered, taken aback by McRookery's outburst of feeling. "Of course it will."

"Let's go, then!" McRookery commanded, and Tony saw them go back the way they had come.

Only then did he let himself take a deep breath. His head was spinning. What had McRookery just said? "Turn the cemetery into a garden" and "the end of that rabble of vampires" – was that just wishful thinking, or was it already a well-thought-out plan? Tony wasn't sure. But one thing was clear: the vampires must be warned!

And only one person could do that – he, Tony!

Visiting the Invalid

Tony plucked up his courage and crept through the long grass to the entrance hole. There he pushed aside the mossy stone, looked round carefully once more and, when he couldn't see anything suspicious, he slid feet first down into the dark hole. He had hardly landed at the bottom when he heard a bright voice calling, "Who's that?"

It was Anna.

"It's me, Tony!" he called, and pulled the stone back over the hole.

"Tony?" Anna sounded surprised. "What are you doing here?"

"I've come to see you," he answered and ran down the steps into the vault.

The stub of a candle flickered on the wall, and by its light, he could see Anna lying in her coffin. Her small, pale face was drawn, and her skin looked almost transparent.

"Anna!" Happy, but worried, he went over to her.

"I'm – I'm not well," she said defensively and lowered her eyes.

Tony picked up her cold little hand and gave it a squeeze. "Don't you feel a little bit better?"

"A bit," she murmured, but it didn't sound very convincing.

"I just wanted to tell you how – how sorry I am." How difficult it was to say things like that! Tony gave an embarrassed little cough.

Anna smiled weakly and looked up at him. "Thank you," she said softly, and Tony saw that her eyes were swollen and inflamed.

"Is there anything I can do to help?" he asked sympathetically.

"Help? I don't know – yes, perhaps . . ."

"How?"

"There are drops – I've heard Aunt Dorothy talking about them."

"Eye-drops?"

"Aunt Dorothy called them Devil's Tears."

"And they would help?"

"Yes. But I don't know where to get them from."

"Can't you ask Aunt Dorothy?"

"No." She shook her head. "Then it would all come out. You know we vampires aren't allowed to make friends with humans."

"Of course!" said Tony. The Little Vampire had already been banished from the vault once before as a punishment for being friendly with him.

"Perhaps you could get them from a doctor?" he suggested.

"Do you think so?" she said doubtfully.

"Yes, why not?" The more he thought about it, the better the idea seemed. "Haven't you heard how many medicines there are at the moment? It's called the pharmaceutical flood."

"The what?"

"Nowadays there's a special medicine for each and

every illness. Why shouldn't there be Devil's Tears as well?"

A glimmer of hope showed on Anna's face.

"If only it were really true . . ."

"Don't the others look after you at all?" Tony looked round the vault. The lids of the coffins were pushed untidily to the side, as if all the other vampires had got up in a hurry. Only one coffin was still shut: Uncle Theodore's. But Uncle Theodore wasn't one of the – er – living ones any more.

Anna shrugged her shoulders. "That's the way it is with us vampires."

"Rudolph even threw away the carton of milk I wanted to bring you," Tony complained.

"I don't drink milk any more," Anna answered softly.

"Not at all?"

"Not a drop."

Tony felt himself shudder. Anna had been the only one who drank milk from time to time.

"But I would rather starve to death than ever use you . . ." She went red.

"I – er – I must tell you something urgently." Tony hastily changed the subject.

"Yes?" she said expectantly.

"McRookery and Sniveller – I overheard them talking about the cemetery. They want to turn it into a garden!"

Anna gave an involuntary cry of horror. "They said that? You couldn't have misheard them?"

"No."

"Then we must call a family council," she declared, breathing heavily. "It *would* happen just when my eyes – but you'll get the Devil's Tears for me, won't you?" She looked pleadingly at Tony, who felt himself go warm.

"Sure!"

"Right now?" she asked urgently.

Tony looked at her in surprise. But today's Saturday, he wanted to say, then he changed his mind and said, "OK, if you like."

"Of course I'd like them now!" she cried. "My whole life as a vampire may depend on those Devil's Tears."

"Then I'll go straight away," Tony murmured, feeling ashamed that he had raised false hopes. The earliest he could possibly go to Dr Dozee to get the drops would be Monday morning. But this way at least he would get out of the vault quickly – before any of the other vampires came back. Anna would have to help him climb out . . .

"What are you waiting for?" she asked, as he stayed standing by her coffin.

In a small voice he said, "I'll – I'll never manage on my own."

"What?"

"To climb out of the hole."

"Oh, I see. Then you must use the emergency exit."

"Where's that?"

Anna laughed softly, and pointed to Uncle Theodore's coffin. "Over there. You'll have to lift the lid."

"Then what?"

"Then you'll see."

Reluctantly, Tony went over to the big, black coffin. An engraved letter T, framed by two snakes, did not exactly tempt him to go further. But he pulled himself together and tugged at the two golden handles as hard as he could.

At first nothing happened. Then it gave a jerk and the heavy lid slid to one side.

"Well?" Anna called excitedly. "Can you see the emergency exit?"

"No. Everything's pitch black."

"Then take the candle from the wall."

"The candle?" Tony turned round hesitatingly. He wasn't sure he wanted to see the inside of the coffin as clearly as all that.

"Yes. You'll have to have some light in any case when you go through the emergency exit. It's pitch black through there, or at any rate it is for you humans."

"Won't you need the candle?" Tony asked, still undecided.

She shook her head sadly. "No. After all, I can't read."

Tony fetched the candle and, with mixed feelings, shone the light into Uncle Theodore's coffin.

At first, all he could see were thick layers of dust and a couple of dead spiders. But at the top end of the coffin he could make out a passage leading sharply downwards into the earth – not very inviting, he thought to himself.

"I . . . I don't know," he murmured.

"There's no need to worry that it'll cave in," Anna reassured him.

"I'm not worried. But suppose I meet someone coming in the other direction – like Aunt Dorothy?"

"You won't. It's strictly forbidden to use it as an entrance to the vault."

"Really?" said Tony, now slightly more confident.

"Yes," came the answer out of the darkness in the vault. After a pause, she added, "And anyway, I think it's important that you know about our emergency exit – now that things have come to a head with McRookery and Sniveller."

"That's true," Tony nodded. "Then – then I'll be off."

"Good luck!" she called softly. "And don't forget the Devil's Tears!"

Tony climbed into the coffin, pulled the lid back over him and crept into the tunnel.

The Emergency Exit

Tony moved forward as carefully as he could, trying not to let the candle go out. Its feeble little light shuddered and spluttered, but held fast.

That gave Tony courage and he started to look curiously around him.

The walls had been neatly smoothed. In several places, someone had scratched something on them. Tony noticed a large 'G', then a mouth showing pointed vampire teeth, and finally a heart with "A + T" engraved within it. The heart must have been Anna's handiwork. And Tony could well imagine whom she meant by the A and the T. He scratched a fat question mark with his fingernail beside it.

The passage was becoming narrower. It could not be far to the end now. Tony could tell from the gust of air coming towards him, making his candle's flame splutter more than ever. Then the flame suddenly went out, and Tony was left in utter blackness.

After a moment, his eyes grew used to the dark. In front of him he could see a feeble glimmer of light, which seemed to be coming through a crevice. As he moved nearer, he could see that a stone lay across the exit, and light was filtering in on either side of it.

31

It must be a gravestone in the cemetery. It felt as cold as marble, and it was so heavy that Tony could only push it a centimetre at a time to one side. Finally he succeeded. He slipped past it – and let out a yell of fright: before him lay an abyss, a black hole full of water.

He could see stone walls overgrown with moss, and a narrow ladder leading upwards. And suddenly he knew where he was: at the bottom of an old well.

Fearfully, he peered down at the water, which gurgled gently, reflecting the moon. What if he'd fallen in? But perhaps it wasn't as deep as all that. He found a piece of gravel and plopped it into the water. Almost immediately, he heard a clinking noise. He let out the breath he had been holding. The water couldn't be more than knee-deep. He might have figured that out, he thought to himself. Anna would never have let him stumble off into disaster without warning him.

Tony gave the ladder a little shake. It was made of iron, rather rusty, but still firmly anchored to the wall. He pulled himself up and started to climb, rung after rung, to the top. He didn't look back once, for fear of getting dizzy and tumbling back down the well. He had once read about a man to whom that had happened. When at last Tony reached the top of the well, he heaved a deep sigh.

Just a few steps away he could see the old chapel. McRookery would often potter about happily in it, and Tony guessed it was here that he stored his tools for his campaign against the vampires: his wooden stakes, his hammer and his stock of garlic. Tony had better make himself scarce in case McRookery suddenly popped up. He spread out his arms under his cloak and flew away.

When he arrived home, he was relieved to find that

his parents still had not come back from their visit to the Dozees. He quickly hid the cloak in his cupboard and put on his pyjamas. Then he fell into bed, turned his head to the wall, and was asleep in an instant.

A New Excuse

Sunday morning . . . Tony woke up and blinked. He had the feeling he was surfacing from a long way away. Through a sort of haze, he could see someone standing by his bed – it was Mum.

He closed his eyes tightly again and grumbled. "Why have you woken me up so early?"

"Early?" She gave a scornful laugh. "Other families have probably finished lunch by now."

"How late is it, then?"

"Half past twelve."

Tony jumped up in alarm. Half past twelve – that was a new record for him.

"What was going on here yesterday evening?" His mother's voice sounded as though she was not going to be put off the scent.

"Here? What do you mean?"

"You went out, didn't you?"

Tony scratched his head. "Mmm – yeah." He had no idea how she knew, but there was obviously no point in lying about it. "I needed some fresh air."

"Fresh air – I see," she retorted hotly. "That's a new one!"

"I had a headache."

"Shall I tell you what *I* think?" Her eyes were blazing as she looked at him. Tony turned to jelly. "I think you went out to meet your friends."

"Which friends?"

"Those – those vampires! What other reason would you have for wandering around outside in the dark?"

Tony had no idea what to say. For want of something to do, he started to scratch his head.

"For goodness sake, stop scratching!' Mum exclaimed irritably. "Tell me instead how your shoes got this filthy and your trousers got covered in dirt."

She seized Tony's shoes, which were lying over by the window, and his trousers, which he had chucked on the floor, and waved them in front of his nose. Tony realized with a shock that they looked as if he'd been wallowing in mud.

"I . . ." he began hesitantly.

"Yes?" she demanded.

Tony turned first red, then white, under her piercing gaze. Suddenly he had a brilliant idea – an idea that he hadn't tried out as an excuse before.

"I was training for the Sports Gala!"

"The Sports Gala?" She stared at him in utter amazement.

"Yes! Our Sports Gala's on Friday, and I've got to practise for it."

"And just exatly why did you have to practise on a Saturday night when it's dark?"

"Ah," he said slowly, "the programmes on television were so boring." Then something else occurred to him. "Oh, by the way, I drank a carton of milk too, preparing for the Sports Gala – I might get a certificate. You'd like me to win a certificate, wouldn't you?"

His mother gave him a withering glance. She felt

certain Tony was not telling her the whole truth, but of course she had no way of proving it.

"There's breakfast on the kitchen table," she said, and added sarcastically, "Sports fanatic!"

"Coming!" Tony grinned. "I must get fit and strong for Friday!"

In fact, he couldn't stand sports galas. All that stupid cross-country running, jumping into sandpits and chucking wobbly rubber balls through the air – it was just not his idea of fun. The only good thing about it was that on the day of the Sports Gala lessons were off!

The Prescription

Tony had a day off school on Monday. There he was, without a bite of breakfast, sitting in Dr Dozee's surgery in a grumpy mood, watching as the nurse drew blood from his arm. She did it very efficiently and it hardly hurt at all.

"What exactly do you do with the blood?" he wanted to know.

"We'll test it," came the reply.

"And then what?"

"It gets thrown away."

"What a shame!"

"A shame?" She raised her head and studied Tony, half in amusement, half in surprise. "Do you know of a use for it?"

"Me?" Tony grinned. "Why should I?"

The nurse pulled the needle out of his arm and it pricked.

"Ouch!" Tony cried.

"Was it that bad?" asked the nurse.

"Oh, I'm used to pain," he said.

She laughed. "That's all right, then. See you next time."

"I hope there won't be a next time," said Tony, and he

trotted into the consulting room, where his mother was already sitting beside Dr Dozee's desk.

"Ah! Here comes our sportsman!" Dr Dozee greeted him.

"Sportsman?" Tony growled, rubbing the plaster that covered his puncture mark.

"Your mother was telling me how keen you've been to practise for the Sports Gala."

"Ah, I see . . ."

Dr Dozee smiled at Tony and pointed to a chair facing her desk. "Come and sit down."

Reluctantly, Tony sat down in the padded chair. He had the feeling he was in for a long and gruelling interrogation.

Dr Dozee clicked her ballpoint pen. "Now, Tony, tell me how you've been doing?"

"Me? Everything's fine!"

"No problems at all?" Once again, she made her pen go click.

"Sometimes my eyes hurt a bit," said Tony, hoping he would not blush.

He saw his mother and Dr Dozee exchange glances.

"Your eyes?" Dr Dozee repeated. "What sort of trouble are you having with them?"

"Well . . ."

Tony had carefully thought out what he would say before he arrived, but it was going to be more difficult to trick a doctor than he'd thought.

"They burn so much. And just recently I haven't been able to read properly in school because they're so itchy."

"Why haven't you told me all this?" Mum exclaimed reproachfully.

"I – er, it only happens sometimes, and then I forget."

Dr Dozee wrote something down. Then she stood up.

"I think we'll have a look at them."

"It won't hurt, will it?" Tony cried.

"No."

He had to look from side to side, and then up and down.

"I can't see anything unusual there," said Dr Dozee. "Perhaps you've been reading too much."

"Yes – those wretched vampire stories!" said Mum angrily.

"Vampire stories?" Dr Dozee pricked up her ears. Turning to Tony, she asked, "Do you like reading that sort of book?"

Tony could not help it, he had to grin. "Yes."

"And do you believe that vampires exist in real life?"

"No one believes that!" said Tony, grinning again.

His answer seemed to reassure Dr Dozee. She nodded to Tony's mother and said, "You see – he's well able to tell the difference between fantasy and reality."

She wrote down something else and then handed Tony a piece of paper. It was a prescription.

"For your eyes," she explained. "I've prescribed some drops for you. You should take them as soon as your eyes begin to burn."

Tony gazed fixedly at the prescription and tried to read her handwriting. The first letter just might be a D.

With a beating heart, he enquired, "What's the name of these drops?" It was a bit cheeky, but he simply had to know.

"Tulli-Ex," Dr Dozee answered.

"Tulli-Ex?" Tony repeated in disappointment.

"Did you want a different kind?" asked Dr Dozee in surprise.

"Um – would you be able to prescribe Devil's Tears for me?"

"What did you say? Devil's Tears?" Dr Dozee gave an uncomfortable laugh. "I've never heard of them. No, no, you use Tulli-Ex like a good boy. They're not too strong, and most people get on well with them."

"Devil's Tears?" said Tony's mother irritably. "I'm sure they're something you've read about in one of your horror stories."

Dr Dozee laid the ballpoint pen down on the desk in front of her. The appointment had obviously come to an end. Tony felt the tension go out of his body.

"What about the blood test?" asked his mother.

"I won't have the result till tomorrow. Give me a call then." Dr Dozee stood up and so did Tony, feeling relieved.

"Good. I'll ring you tomorrow then." From his mother's sour expression, Tony guessed she had hoped for more from this visit to the doctor.

Oh, well, Tony thought gleefully, you should always be prepared for disappointments!

He found out just how right he was when, as soon as they were in the car, his mother announced, "Well, that's the end of all that reading, my boy – and the end of so much television, too!"

"Why?" Tony cried furiously.

She lifted the prescription out of the glove compartment and waved it in front of Tony's face.

"This is why."

Tony bit his lip and said nothing.

What he had to put up with – and all for Anna! As they drove along, he wondered what other ways there might be of getting hold of Devil's Tears. Perhaps he could ask the science teacher, or look them up in an encyclopedia, or ask about them in a bookshop, or even ring up a newspaper. None of these ideas seemed very promising.

Suddenly his mother pulled up to the kerb and stopped. Tony gave a start, and noticed a large sign that said: CHEMIST. Of course! Now why hadn't he thought of that himself?

Quickly, he snatched the prescription and opened the door of the car.

"I'll get it!" he said.

"You?" said Mum in surprise.

"Why not?" Tony grinned, and got out.

Thank goodness his mother stayed where she was and didn't try to come in with him!

He went into the chemist's shop in a state of some agitation. It was empty, except for a kind-looking man in a white coat who was standing behind the counter, writing something down in a ledger.

He did not look up until Tony had put the prescription down on the counter. Then he fetched a packet from one of the shelves – the name Tulli-Ex stood out clearly in large letters on the front of it – and put it in front of Tony. But Tony did not move.

"Did you want anything else?" asked the chemist, sounding rather puzzled.

Tony cleared his throat. "I – er – Tulli-Ex are eye-drops, aren't they?"

"Yes."

"Would you recommend them? I mean, would you take them yourself if you —"

"Why ever not?"

"It's just that —" Tony took a deep breath. "There are some very special drops my friend told me about . . ."

"Yes, well?" The chemist was staring at him with open curiosity.

"They're called Devil's Tears," said Tony.

"Devil's Tears?" The chemist laughed, and Tony could

41

see his large yellow teeth. "Never heard of 'em. They're supposed to be eye-drops, are they?"

Tony nodded.

"I'll look it up on the computer." The chemist switched on the screen of his terminal. After a while he said, "Just as I thought. Devil's Tears don't exist. Your friend's been pulling your leg." He pointed to the Tulli-Ex. "Try these instead."

"OK. Thanks."

Tony put the packet into his pocket and went out. Poor Anna! he thought.

Tulli-Ex

Once back in his room, Tony opened the packet and took out the little bottle. It was made of clear plastic. Carefully he let a couple of drops of the colourless liquid drip on his hand, and sniffed them. Tulli-Ex did not smell of anything. Were Devil's Tears like that, with no colour and no smell? How silly of him not to have asked Anna! Otherwise, he could have simply given her the Tulli-Ex and told her it was Devil's Tears. If Anna had believed him, the Tulli-Ex drops probably would have helped her eyes.

Tony pulled a closely printed slip of paper out of the packet and tried to read what was in Tulli-Ex. It was full of strange words and it was all written in a very complicated way. But even so, Tony could understand that Tulli-Ex drops were especially mild and could be used for all types of eye trouble, from tired, inflamed eyes to conjunctivitis. He did not know which infection Anna had, but surely Tulli-Ex could not do her any harm!

He studied the bottle thoughtfully from every side, and suddenly he had an idea. All he needed to do was remove the label saying "Tulli-Ex". After that, no one would be able to say for sure what sort of drops the bottle contained. And it might even be possible to make Anna believe they were her precious Devil's Tears.

Tony knew how to remove a label from the time when he had been interested in stamp collecting. He went into the bathroom and fetched a bowl of water. Then he screwed the cap firmly back on the bottle and laid it in the warm water. Finally, he put his atlas over the top of it. It was vital that Mum didn't get wind of any of this.

The rest of the day passed rather drearily. Just as his mother had said. Tony was not allowed to read or watch television. When it grew dark, he put on his track-suit, stuck the Tulli-Ex in his pocket and went into the living-room.

His parents were glued to the television, of course. They were watching some pathetic family serial.

"I see you're watching the Peasbody family and their friends!" Tony said with a grin.

His mother looked up. "Have you used your eye drops?"

"Yes. Can I go out for a bit?"

"Now? It's pitch dark outside!"

"But I must practise for the Sports Gala." He bit his lip, as he always did when he was trying not to laugh. "And it's not as dark as all that. I'll only run along the streets that have streetlighting."

"Why didn't you go running this afternoon while it was still light?"

"I was training in my room," said Tony. "Knee-bends and – what do you call them? – mess-ups."

"Press-ups!" Dad corrected. "Well, I think it's excellent that Tony is at last showing some interest in physical exercise. Why shouldn't he go for a run a couple of times round the block? After all, he's not a baby any more."

"Quite!" said Tony happily.

"All right, if you say so," said Mum.

"See you later!" Tony did a couple of knee-bends just to show how sporty he was, then made for the door.

Once in the lift, he took the Tulli-Ex out of his pocket. If he was lucky, he would bump into the Little Vampire and give him the drops to take to Anna.

An Unexpected Meeting

Out on the pavement in front of the building, Tony did some exercises he had been taught in PE: bending his body, wiggling his toes, circling his arms and hopping. While he went through all this, he was squinting up at the flat. It was always possible that his parents might be watching him. He had the impression that the blinds at the kitchen window did move slightly, but he could not be sure. Then he set off.

A fat man carrying a briefcase was walking towards him, and stepped reluctantly aside.

"Hey, young man, this isn't a sports field, you know!" he grumbled.

"Isn't it?" said Tony and, as he ran past, he bumped into him accidentally-on-purpose.

"Hooligan! Wait till I catch you!" the man cried, and ran a couple of paces after Tony, but of course he had no chance of catching up with him.

"You should take some exercise like me!" Tony called back to him with a broad grin.

"Just you wait, you little blighter!" The man came to a stop, gasping for breath. "One day I'll get hold of you and then . . ."

What he would do then, Tony never found out,

because he had crossed the street and nipped down a path bordered by shrubs and trees. He stopped behind a bush to catch his breath. He had a painful stitch, a sign that he wasn't in very good shape. But he'd been fit enough to get away from the fat man. People like that always thought they owned everything: the pavement, the street, the whole world, even! Those blokes with briefcases really got up Tony's nose.

"Bravo! Well done!" said a hoarse voice suddenly from nearby.

Tony spun round – and saw Gregory!

"I would never have thought it of you!"

"Wh–what?" Tony stuttered, taking a step backwards.

Gregory's face was a mass of little red spots, like a currant bun. On his chin, between the sparse, unshaven bristles, he sported a large, blood-stained plaster – eeugh!

"I'd never have thought you'd have the guts!" Gregory explained, taking two paces nearer to Tony. "The way you knocked into that fat guy – it was brilliant! You're not afraid of anything, man or beast, are you?" He placed his huge, strong hands on Tony's shoulders. "How nice to see you again!" he growled, showing Tony his spotless teeth.

"Y-yes, you t-too!" Tony stammered, trying to wriggle out of Greg's grip. But he was held as firmly as if in a vice.

"You're looking better than you used to!" Greg studied him with gleaming eyes, letting his gaze wander slowly over Tony's face, then down to his neck. "You're looking very healthy!"

"Do you think so? My mother wouldn't agree with you."

"Wouldn't she?" It was obvious that Greg did not believe a word of it. "What does your mummy say?"

"She even made me go to the doctor!"

"Doctors – pooh, rubbish!" Gregory opened his gaping mouth. "She'd have done better to have sent you to me."

And, with a longing look at Tony's neck, he added, "Just one teeny-weeny bite from me can work wonders, I can tell you!"

An icy dread ran through Tony. He shrugged his shoulders and said coolly, "Well, I'm anaemic!"

"What? Anaemic?" Greg shrieked, and spat on the ground. "That's the most tiresome, unnecessary illness I've ever heard of!" He spat again, in disgust. Then his face took on a hard, cunning expression and, with a large wink, he announced, "One thing I don't believe is that *you*'ve got it!"

Tony struggled to keep calm. "Why not? The doctor even did a blood test on me."

"A blood test?" Gregory repeated, listening carefully to the sound of the words. Then his mood changed again and he thundered, "Why the doctor? I can test your blood just as well myself."

To his dismay, Tony saw that Greg's eyes were getting the fixed gaze that vampires use to hypnotize their victims. Now was the moment to act!

Swiftly, Tony pulled the Tulli-Ex out of his pocket and held it right under Greg's nose. Greg gave an irritated snort.

"What on earth's that?" he growled.

"They're drops – for Anna!"

"Anna, Anna . . ." Greg murmured dully. "Right now there's no such person as Anna. There's just the two of us – you and me!" He uttered a deep, throaty growl – like a wild animal, Tony thought with a shudder – then he opened his enormous mouth and leaned forward to sink his teeth into Tony's neck.

At the last moment, Tony jammed the bottle of Tulli-Ex between his teeth. Greg's jaws closed round the bottle with a sharp clunk.

For a second or two, Greg stayed motionless. Gradually, he seemed to realize that something was not quite right. He opened his mouth and the Tulli-Ex fell out.

"What happened?" he asked, puzzled.

"I wanted to give you Anna's drops," said Tony hastily, picking the bottle up off the ground.

Gregory was obviously confused and, taking advantage of this, Tony pressed the Tulli-Ex into his hand, saying, "Here, these are Anna's drops!"

Greg just stood there stupefied, his eyes glassy and vacant. It gave Tony a strange feeling to see him in such a state. He knew Greg was one of the most dangerous and unpredictable of the vampires, and suddenly he was letting Tony give him the Tulli-Ex without a murmur, holding on to the bottle like a good, obedient schoolboy. Perhaps it was all because of the Tulli-Ex drops? Perhaps Greg had got some in his mouth and they had made him a bit tipsy? Or did vampires always get like this when they thought they . . . er . . . had a victim in their clutches?

Tony didn't know.

But it was quite obvious that he must not hang around a minute longer. The moment Gregory woke up from this trance, he would be bound to go for Tony's throat – literally!

Once more Tony urged, "Don't forget the drops! They're for Anna, and they're very important!"

Then he took to his heels. He ran the whole length of the path without looking round. As he reached the street, he heard a hoarse roaring sound behind him.

"Tony? Where are you?" It was Greg's voice and he sounded furious.

He had obviously come round. Tony ran as fast as he

could. At this rate, I'll break every record at the Sports Gala! he thought, as he finally reached home, totally out of breath.

"You seem to be training for the Olympics!' his father teased.

"No!" Tony gasped. "That was survival training!"

"Survival training?" Mum repeated disapprovingly. "Now you're falling for every craze that's going!"

"*I* am?" Tony retorted, fixing his eyes on her new mid-calf boots with a grin. She went a bit red – and quickly turned back to the television programme.

Being Clean

"I'm going to bed now!" Tony announced.

"What? Like that?" asked Mum sharply.

Tony looked down. His track-suit was damp with sweat and clung to his body.

"No. I'll take my track-suit off."

"That's not what I meant!"

"And my trainers!" he added grumpily. "May I go to my room now?"

"No!"

"Why not?"

"Because you're going to the bathroom first!"

"Then why didn't you say so in the first place?" Tony groused.

"And there you'll have a shower!"

"A shower? But it's so late!"

"Oh yes, the two things definitely go together," Dad put in. "E and S is every sportsman's motto!"

"E and S?" Tony growled. What on earth was he going on about now?

"Exercise and shower!" his father explained, breaking into peals of self-satisfied laughter.

Tony did not find his remark in the least bit funny, but he could not think of a suitable retort, so he went into the bathroom. As he undressed, he wondered whether to have a shower, or whether just to let the water run. But his mother was bound to check the towels and it was probably simpler just to get into the shower straight away.

When he felt the warm stream of water flowing over his skin, he found he was actually enjoying it. He began to sing.

"Oh, the good ship sailed on the alley, alley-o!" he sang at the top of his voice, till someone next door banged on the wall and yelled something that Tony could not understand.

Tony turned off the shower and shouted back, "You're right, I don't think much of being clean either!"

At that moment, the bathroom door opened.

"Have you gone mad?" Mum scolded. "Do you want the neighbours to come and blow us up?"

"Blow us up?" said Tony with a grin, looking at the ceiling. "That wouldn't do their flat much good either, would it?"

His mother shut the door crossly.

"Oh, well," said Tony, slinging a towel round his shoulders, "some people are never satisfied!"

He set off for his bedroom, but his mother suddenly came pushing past him.

"Your window's wide open," she said, disappearing into his room.

"What? My window's open?" Tony cried, and he began to shiver exaggeratedly. "I'll catch pneumonia!"

"There was that horrible smell in your room again," Mum explained, tugging the window shut. "If only I could find out where it's coming from!"

Tony knew exactly what was making the stink: the vampire cloak in his cupboard.

But it was true, today the smell was particularly strong. Although the window had been wide open till a moment before, the room was already beginning to smell like a hyena's den.

"Perhaps you've got an old pair of dirty socks in your cupboard?" asked Mum, moving towards it as if to open the door.

"Stop!" Tony cried.

She hesitated. "Why can't I look in your cupboard?"

"Because – there are presents in there that I'm making for you both."

"Presents?"

"Yes. For Christmas."

Today was only 22 October, but still.

"Some people start getting ready for Christmas early," Tony declared with a cheeky grin. Whether she believed him or not, at least he had put her off rummaging through his cupboard.

"All right, you have a look yourself then," she said, "and I bet you'll unearth at least four pairs of dirty socks – from the smell, it might be more like fifty!" she added sharply, as she left the room.

"Dirty socks indeed!" Tony growled. "Now where am I going to magic those up from?"

"Here are some socks if you need some!" came a rasping voice, and Tony saw a skinny hand appear from under his bed, holding out a pair of holey black socks.

"Is – is that you, Rudolph?" he stammered.

"Yes." The hand with the socks shot back again. "But don't give me away!"

"What are you doing under there?"

"I've got to talk to you."

"In a m-minute." It had been such a shock to the system to find Rudolph there that Tony's heart was still hammering unevenly. "First I've got to find some socks to give Mum."

"If you give me some clean ones, you can have mine," the vampire offered with a husky laugh.

"Clean socks? No problem!" Tony went over to his cupboard. There lay plenty of socks, all neatly rolled up in pairs. "What colour would you like?"

"Black. No – red, blood-red!"

Tony threw him a pair of brilliant red ones. He had been given them by Gran, but he had never worn them, because he did not want to look like some sort of red-legged stork.

The vampire gave a whistle. "Cor! They're great!" he crowed, and straight away his black vampire socks landed at Tony's feet.

Tony would have liked a pair of tweezers to pick them up with. He held his nose and groped for them with his fingertips. They were so thick with dirt that they had gone quite stiff, and they stank of . . . well, it was just indescribable!

But more to the point, now he had something to show his mother. He took the socks into the bathroom and dropped them into the laundry basket with a sigh. Then he called over to the living-room, "I've found the socks that were making that smell!"

"Well done!" Mum replied. "Where are they now?"

"In the laundry basket."

"Good. I'll wash them tomorrow. Sleep well."

"Yes. Night."

Something Terrible's Going to Happen!

When Tony came back to his room, Rudolph was nowhere to be seen. He closed the door, and then the Little Vampire emerged from under the bed.

"Has the smell gone?" he asked in his husky voice.

"Yes," said Tony, adding, "'Cause your socks have gone!"

"You're right!" The vampire grinned. He sat on the bed, stretched out both legs and wiggled his toes in their new red socks. "These are really cool – or should I say, hot as hell!"

"I'm sure Olga would have liked them!" Tony teased, remembering Rudolph's old heart-throb.

"Olga?" The vampire sat bolt upright and stared at Tony with blazing eyes. Then he seemed to crumple, and just murmured dully, "Don't talk to me about Olga. You're opening up a wound deep inside me which still hasn't healed."

Tony bit his lip to stop himself laughing. Only Rudolph could have fallen for such a stuck-up, conceited girl-vampire as the Honourable Olga Pigsbubble.

The Little Vampire sniffled and ran a scrawny hand over his eyes. "Let's not talk about the past," he said hoarsely. "The present is bad enough!"

"What do you mean?" asked Tony in concern.

"The cemetery. Something terrible's going to happen!"

"Do you mean what McRookery and Sniveller have in mind?"

The vampire looked at Tony in surprise. "You know about it?"

"I listened to their conversation. They want to turn the cemetery into a garden and then that will be the end, once and for all, to —" Tony stopped.

"To what?" Rudolph demanded.

"To all you vampires."

"That confirms my worst fears!" said the vampire in a voice of doom.

"What's happened?" Tony wanted to know.

"Two huge vehicles have just been brought to the cemetery. And McRookery and Sniveller were standing there rubbing their hands."

"What sort of vehicles?"

"Some sort of earth movers, I think. Do you know much about machines?"

"Mmm – yes."

"Hey, great!" The vampire sounded pleased. "I thought you would. So then you . . ." The vampire gave a meaningful pause.

"What?" Tony asked impatiently.

"Then you must help us!"

"I *must* help you?" Tony repeated, imitating Rudolph's demanding tone. "What if I don't want to?"

Rudolph stared at him in amazement. "Don't you want to?"

"Well, maybe, maybe not!" Tony answered, enjoying the vampire's confusion. Then he added in a very dignified voice, "But I'm not going to be bossed around, especially not by you!"

"I'm – I'm sorry," the vampire stuttered. Then he asked quietly, "But you are still our friend, aren't you?"

"Yes, of course!"

"So could you perhaps, I mean . . . would you perhaps help us . . . please?"

It was quite obvious how difficult it was for the vampire to beg Tony for help. Tony gave a broad grin.

"Since you ask so nicely!"

"Thanks be to Dracula!" said the vampire, sighing with relief.

"What do you want me to do?" asked Tony.

"Well, it would be great if you – if you would go to the cemetery tomorrow afternoon and see what you can find out for us."

"You want me to hang around listening?"

"Well, you're a human, aren't you? No one will suspect anything."

"Do you really think so?"

"Sure. All you've got to do is take a watering can and a little rake with you, and no one will even notice you."

"I'll think about it," Tony mumbled.

Rudolph looked at him pleadingly. "Please!"

"Oh, all right then!" Tony was flattered.

"I'll come and see you tomorrow evening." The vampire slipped on his shoes and climbed on to the windowsill.

"Hey, what's the hurry?" asked Tony.

The vampire grinned. "Can't you hear?"

"No. What?"

"My stomach's rumbling!" said the vampire and swept off into the night with a throaty chuckle.

58

Don't Get Your Knickers in a Twist!

The next morning, Tony was woken up very roughly. His mother marched into his room, switched on the light and asked, "Where on earth have these disgusting things come from?"

Tony blinked. "Hey, turn the light off!"

"Only when you've told me who these horrible objects belong to!"

"What objects?" Tony opened one eye carefully, although he did not actually need to because he could already smell what his mother was dangling under his nose: Rudolph's black socks!

"What do you mean?" he asked innocently. "I thought you wanted me to sort out my dirty socks."

His mother dropped the socks in disgust. "Yours? These filthy, stinking things never, ever belonged to you!"

"But they do!" Tony protested. "They do now!"

"What do you mean – now?"

"I – we – swopped."

"Who did? Now I really must get to the bottom of this!"

Tony groaned softly. He had hardly woken up and already he was expected to answer all these questions!

"Me and Rudolph," he said. "I gave him some of my socks, and he gave me a pair of his."

"You call these socks?" his mother exclaimed. "They're more holes than socks!" She shook her head angrily. "Which socks did you give to Rudolph?"

"The red ones."

"Not the ones Gran gave you?"

"Now don't get your knickers in a twist!"

"I'm not talking about knickers – I'm talking about socks! I just don't believe it! You swop your new socks for these!" She nudged Rudolph's socks with her toe and made a face. "They stink! I was nearly sick when I went into the bathroom."

Tony giggled. "You wanted dirty socks – and you got them!"

His mother laughed loftily. "Do you really think I'm going to bother to put these rags in the washing machine?"

"Why not?" asked Tony. "I can't wear them if they're as dirty as that!"

"You're not going to wear them at all!" Mum retorted. She bent down and, with a look of utter disgust, picked up the socks. Then she went over to the door.

"What are you going to do with them?" Tony cried. He had not actually planned ever to wear them, but he wanted to keep them. After all, they were genuine vampire socks! But they would have to be washed first.

"I'm going to throw them away!" Mum declared.

"Throw them away? What if Rudolph doesn't agree?"

She gave him a scornful look over one shoulder. "I thought you said he'd given them to you?"

"Yes, but —"

"And if Rudolph needs new socks, I'll gladly take him shopping for some."

"I wouldn't do that."

"Why not?"

"Because Rudolph never washes his feet!"

That was too much for Mum. She gave a furious snort and slammed the door behind her.

Tony jumped out of bed, flung open the window and took a couple of deep breaths. Phew! That was better after that fug! Then he got dressed and went out into the hall. His mother was standing by the mirror, buttoning up her coat.

"Are you going already?" he asked in surprise.

"Yes. I want to call in on Dr Dozee quickly before school."

"What are you going to Dr Dozee for?"

"To see if she's received the result of your blood test." She went to the front door. "Any objections?"

"Me?" said Tony, trying not to let her see how pleased he was. "No, none!"

But his mother was cleverer than he'd thought.

"If you think you can rummage about for those revolting socks the moment my back is turned, you can think again," she said, pointing to a bin liner next to her briefcase. "I'm taking the socks with me and they're going in the litter bin!"

"Rudolph's socks? In a litter bin?"

She nodded. "We aren't turning into rag-and-bone men!"

Tony bit his lip in annoyance. Then he said, "If we're on the subject of hoarding things, I know one thing you can save."

"What's that?"

He grinned. "You can save yourself the trouble of going to Dr Dozee."

Now it was her turn to be annoyed.

"We'll just wait and see about that!" she said.

More Difficulties

Tony turned out to be right: there was nothing wrong with his blood.

"You're a hundred per cent healthy," his mother announced at lunch. From the way she said it, Tony guessed she was not too pleased with the result.

"A hundred per cent healthy," he repeated cheerfully. "I told you so." He helped himself to some more potato, so she could see that his appetite was "healthy" too. He added happily, with his mouth full, "You see! The whole stupid examination was a waste of time."

"I wouldn't agree with you there," his mother answered.

"Why not?"

"Dr Dozee has referred us to a psychologist."

"Wha-at?" The potato almost stuck in Tony's throat.

"Tomorrow afternoon we're going to see a psychologist – that's a doctor who looks after your mind. I've already telephoned to make an appointment."

"What?" Tony cried again. "Without asking me first?"

His mother smiled coolly. "Do you know what a psychologist is, exactly?"

"Of course I do – I've seen them on television." Then he added furiously, "And I'm in no mood to have this –

this psychowotsit nosing about in my head!"

Mum laughed. "It won't be as bad as all that! And in any case, I'll be there with you."

Tony pushed his plate away. It still had half a helping on it, but his appetite had completely disappeared. He stood up.

"Where are you going?" Mum cried.

"I'm emigrating!" he growled.

Once in his room, he tried to think about what he had just heard. Psychologists – they were the ones who poked their noses in other people's business, the know-alls who thought the secret of wisdom belonged to them. And now Mum wanted to drag him off to see one. He really had better emigrate! But where would he go? Nowadays, it wasn't even safe in the Sackville-Bagg family vault!

Then he remembered the promise he had made to the Little Vampire. His bucket and spade must still be somewhere around . . .

He had a look and finally found them behind the pile of old comics in his cupboard. Then he crept on tiptoe to the front door. He heard music coming from the kitchen. Without his mother noticing, he opened the door and pulled it shut behind him.

He did not usually go sneaking out like this, but after all, Mum had made a sneaky phone call herself to the psychologist without talking to him about it first. Tony fetched his bike from the basement, strapped the bucket and spade to the carrier and rode off. He hoped he would not meet any of his school friends on the way – otherwise there would be only one topic of conversation in class tomorrow: Tony still likes playing with sand!

The Wreckers of the Environment

As it happened, he was lucky. Apart from an elderly couple dressed in black, he did not meet anybody. He left his bike by the cemetery wall and went in through the gate, which was standing wide open.

The cemetery looked even more desolate today than usual. Instead of the colourful bunches of flowers left there in the summer, the graves were marked only by dismal little evergreen plants, and most of the trees and shrubs were bare of leaves. Tony could even see the outlines of McRookery's house through the hedge. And he could see something else too . . . something large and yellow behind the old chapel.

That must be the earth movers! As he slowly approached the chapel, two engines suddenly spluttered into life with an ear-splitting roar. A horrible bluish cloud of exhaust fumes wafted over Tony. He coughed. Obviously nothing was going to hold back these wreckers of the environment, not even respect for the resting place of the dead.

Of course, all the noise they were making gave him one advantage: no one noticed when he ran round the edge of the chapel and crouched down behind a section of wall that stuck out. Now he was able to look out over the back part of the cemetery without being discovered himself.

And what he saw going on there made his hair stand on end. A huge digger was about to start carving up the earth. All the tombstones and crosses that it had just unearthed were being pushed into a heap by a bulldozer. All the ancient, wild part of the cemetery was being turned into a building site!

Only a couple of trees had been spared. Tony recognized the tall yew tree: under it lay the entrance to the Sackville-Bagg vault.

Now the digger was driving over to the yew tree. It stopped, lowered its grabber, and lifted up a flat stone covered in moss. It was the stone the vampires used to close the entrance to their vault. Now the tunnel would be obvious, open to anyone . . . If McRookery and Sniveller discovered the entrance that would be the end of the vampires!

Tony felt as if something was squeezing his chest. For there were McRookery and Sniveller, running around behind the bulldozer, as happy and excited as a couple of children. But they hadn't noticed the vault . . . not yet, anyway. They were watching the mossy stone as it landed on the ground near the other tombstones. For the moment, the vampires were safe – but for how long?

Tony's hands clenched in powerless anger. When he thought of how the vampires had to lie there underground, utterly helpless in their coffins, unable even to lift a finger till the sun went down! McRookery and Sniveller had machines and workmen. The vampires had no one to help – only him, Tony!

But what could he do, alone against four grown-up men, a digger and a bulldozer? He was powerless, utterly powerless!

Then again, perhaps he wasn't . . .

Suddenly the engines were switched off, the drivers climbed down and in the silence Tony heard one say, "Coffee break!"

They walked directly towards Tony, who shrank back behind the wall. They went past without seeing him, and disappeared inside the chapel. McRookery and Sniveller followed them.

Suddenly Tony found himself alone in the cemetery. He looked over at the tall yew tree, and realized how he could help the vampires.

Off he ran, clutching his bucket and spade in one hand.

Boys Will Be Boys

Tony's first thought was simply to fill up the entrance hole. Then McRookery and Sniveller would never discover it and the vampires could still leave their vault through the emergency exit. But when he reached the entrance hole and looked down into its depths, it was obvious that it would take him hours to fill it in. No, he'd have to do something else . . .

He looked around and saw a tree root that was about the same size as the opening. Putting all his strength into the effort, he managed to heave a large part of it into the hole. The remaining gaps he quickly filled up with earth – and the vault was no more to be seen.

Proud and very relieved, he lifted his head – and found himself staring into McRookery's furious face.

"What do you think you're doing?" McRookery shouted. His short, stubby fingers jerked, as if he were about to pounce on Tony.

"I'm . . . I'm not doing anything!" Tony stammered. He stood up, even though his knees felt like jelly. "I was just playing." He held out the bucket and spade as proof.

"Ah, how sweet!" exclaimed Sniveller, who was standing nearby.

"Sweet?" McRookery turned on him. "The rascal's

poking about all over the place, and you think that's sweet?"

"But I used to love playing in sand like that!" said Sniveller plaintively.

"Playing in sand!" McRookery's eyes were blazing as he stared first at Tony and then at Sniveller. "Can't you see that the lad is far too old for that?" He took a menacing step closer to Tony. "Come on, admit it, you were spying on something!"

Tony took a step backwards, not just because he was a bit scared, but because McRookery stank to high heaven of garlic.

"No!" he protested. "I came because today the sand is being changed in our sandpit at home."

"The sand's being changed?" McRookery looked at him darkly. "Do you take me for an idiot?"

"No, no, he's right, people do change the sand," Sniveller broke in, adding with a giggle, "It's because of the dogs' . . . poos!"

"Huh!" said McRookery furiously. Then he asked gruffly, "And how come you're playing in the cemetery? You should respect the peace and quiet of the dead, you know!"

"Oh, really?" said Tony.

The driver of the bulldozer had just climbed back into his cab.

At that, McRookery grabbed him by the chin and held him tight. "Hey!" he murmured, whistling through his teeth, "I think I know you, my lad!"

"N-no!" Tony stammered. The smell of garlic was so strong, he could hardly breathe.

"Oh yes, I do!" said McRookery in a low, angry voice. "I've seen you round here before."

"Leave him alone, Henry!" Sniveller murmured. "You were a boy once."

At that exact moment, the driver of the digger switched on his engine. A cloud of exhaust fumes enveloped them like a smoke screen. McRookery was standing nearest the exhaust, and he put his hands over his mouth to cough.

Tony took the opportunity to escape. He ran back to the gate, swung himself on to his bike, and sped away.

A Real Nature Conservationalist

Back home, his mother was waiting for him in a reproachful mood. "Since when have you left the flat without letting me know?" she cried.

Tony looked sullen. "Since you started ringing up psychologists behind my back!"

"It's only because we're worried about you."

"Worried? Well, I've got worries of my own!" Tony said gruffly, and he went into his room.

His mother followed him.

"Tony, couldn't we have a grown-up talk about this?"

"About what?" He sat on his bed just as he was, jacket still on and his boots all muddy.

But for once Mum did not scold him. Perhaps she realized that something was not quite right. In an unusually gentle voice, she went on, "About what's worrying you, for instance."

Tony suddenly felt a lump in his throat. In a husky voice he said, "It's those wretched people who are wrecking the environment! They're ruining everything!" He pressed his lips tight together in anger.

"What are they ruining?" she asked.

"Everything!" he repeated, and then added glumly, "The cemetery."

"The cemetery? Are they going to build on it?"

"No. But they've completely flattened that lovely wild bit. They're going to turn it into a park – as if we didn't have enough stupid parks already."

"But surely it doesn't matter to you what happens to the cemetery?" she said with a laugh.

Doesn't matter? If only she knew! Tony thought, but he didn't say anything.

He did not want to be asked any more questions, so he began to take off his boots. He watched with a sort of mischievous glee as little piles of sand appeared on the rug.

"Tony, stop that at once! Your lovely rug!" his mother exclaimed shrilly.

"OK, OK," he replied, pulling and tugging till he had both boots in his hand.

His mother had turned quite pink with anger, and was standing over by the door. "You can clean up that mess yourself," she announced.

"Mess?" said Tony, pushing the sand into one pile. "It's only a little bit of nature! I thought you were all for conserving nature."

Bang! The door slammed shut.

Tony stretched out on his bed and sighed. Once again, he had managed to avoid his mother's tiresome questions, yet he found he was not as pleased as usual. He was far too worried about the vampires.

What would they do now? Perhaps they would even go back to Transylvania. Tony could feel tears welling up in his eyes. And there was nothing he could do about it. He could only hope that, in spite of the dangers hanging over all the vampires, Rudolph would come and see him tonight. If only the time would pass a bit more quickly!

When at last dusk was beginning to fall outside, and

73

Tony was standing expectantly near the window, there came a knock at his bedroom door.

"Tea's ready, Tony!"

"I'm not hungry," he answered.

"Not hungry?" Tony's father peered into the room. "Not even if I tell you I've made fruit salad for us?"

"Fruit salad?" Normally, the thought of it made his mouth water, but he knew that today he would not be able to keep a single mouthful down. "I'll – I'll come in a minute!"

"Don't be too long," Dad warned, "or it'll all be gone!" He closed the door again.

"Let's hope it is all gone," Tony muttered. He stayed by the window, looking at the strange, bluish light. He felt his heart speed up. Now the vampires would be climbing out of their coffins, stretching, yawning, adjusting their cloaks. Tony imagined the first one trying to leave the vault – then discovering that the exit was blocked. Then he heard his mother's voice.

"Tony, we're waiting for you!"

Reluctantly, he trotted off to the kitchen. Unfortunately, the fruit salad was nowhere near finished: there was a big bowl of it, full to the brim, at his place.

"I can't eat all that!" he protested.

"Has the protection of the environment affected your stomach?" Dad teased.

"What do you mean?"

"Mum told me that you've become a nature conservationist."

"So? Is that forbidden?" Tony growled. Unwillingly, he put a piece of apple in his mouth.

"No, of course not. We're pleased you're standing up for nature conservation. It's just – why does it have to be that cemetery again?"

Tony felt his face turning red. "Because no one cares about it apart from me!"

"Is that what you think?" said Dad. "Would you like to hear what it says in the paper?" Without waiting for Tony to reply, he picked up the local paper and started to read:

CEMETERY IMPROVEMENTS

Turning the far side of the cemetery into a park has long been the wish of night-watchman Henry McRookery, aged 59. It is thanks to his tireless efforts that at the last meeting of the budget committee, £2,000 was promised for improvements to the cemetery.

He let the newspaper fall. "You see? It's not true that no one else cares about the cemetery." He looked at the newspaper again. " 'Thanks to his tireless . . .' "

"Yes, thanks to them!" Tony cried, and his voice broke.

"What do you mean?" said his father. "Isn't it a good thing when a bit of waste land, which isn't doing anybody any good, is going to be turned into a lovely park for everyone to enjoy?"

"Not doing anybody any good? How do you know?" Tony was beside himself.

"Do you know someone who's being harmed, then?" Dad asked in amusement.

"Yes, I do! The vam —" Tony cried, and cut himself short in fright. He had come as near as a whisker to giving everything away! "The vo-voles and – and all the other animals that will be driven out of the cemetery."

Dad laughed. "You have turned into a real nature conservationist!"

But Mum looked serious. "I think Tony was about to

75

say something else." She turned to Tony and asked sharply, "You were going to say 'vampires', weren't you?"

"I – I . . ." Tony stammered, turning red again. This time he couldn't think of a way out.

Mum gave a deep sigh. "Thank heavens our appointment with the psychologist is tomorrow. I'm almost at my wits' end with all this!"

"Whitsun?" Tony grinned and stood up. "I thought Whitsun wasn't for another seven months!"

Revenge on the Brain

The Little Vampire was late arriving that evening. Time and again, Tony went over to the window to look out for him – till finally he saw a small black shape flying towards him.

"Rudolph!" he said in relief. "I thought you weren't coming!"

"I almost wasn't!" the vampire growled, gliding into Tony's room. "Everything's topsy-turvy at home. Just imagine: someone's tried to block up our vault, and Aunt Dorothy nearly broke her neck!"

"What?" Tony cried in alarm.

Rudolph nodded. "Our entrance hole was blocked by a tree root. Aunt Dorothy was the first to fly out. She didn't see the root and knocked her head against it."

Tony put his hand to his mouth. "She – she knocked her head on the tree root?" He hadn't thought of that. "Is she badly hurt?"

Now Rudolph gave a grin. "She certainly is. She's got a bump on the head, a blinding headache – and revenge on the brain!"

"Revenge? Revenge on whom?" Tony asked with a shudder.

"On the person who put the tree root over the hole, of

course." Rudolph paused before adding confidentially, "His life's hanging by a thread, and she's going to bite through it!"

"Er – have you any idea who it was?"

"We think it was McRookery."

"McRookery?"

"Yes – who else could it have been?"

"It – it could have been Sniveller." Tony stammered.

"Oh, him!" Rudolph waved his hand scornfully. "He wouldn't touch a dirty old tree root. He'd be too worried about breaking one of his precious fingernails."

At the word "fingernails", Tony glanced down nervously at his own hands – and jumped! There was still a lot of black cemetery earth under his own nails.

He quickly hid his hands in his trouser pockets. But the Little Vampire was much too agitated to be interested in Tony's fingernails.

"Did you go to the cemetery this afternoon?" he asked. Tony nodded.

"Well? Did you find anything out?"

"McRookery nearly caught me when I was —" Tony stopped in fright. He'd nearly given himself away.

"When you were what?" the vampire cried impatiently.

"When I was trying to get a look at the digger."

"Digger! Digger!" The Little Vampire sounded irritated as he mimicked him. "I already know they've got a digger. Didn't you find out anything else?"

"No," said Tony. "Only that they've flattened the whole of the back part of the cemetery."

"I've seen that!" said the vampire indignantly.

"And it says so in the papers," Tony added.

"What?"

"That McRookery's got £2,000 for the cemetery

im —" Tony decided it was better not to use the word "improvements", so as not to make the Little Vampire even angrier.

But before Tony could think of a suitable word, the vampire came to the rescue. "Cemetery elimination, you mean!"

"Exactly!" Tony nodded.

There was a pause. They could hear the sound of the television in the living-room.

"And how are things with you all otherwise?" asked Tony in a strained voice.

"Us?" said the vampire. His deathly pale face, his sunken cheeks and the dark circles under his eyes made him suddenly look very tired. "We'll manage somehow. We always have," he said gloomily. Then he added, "Don't think it's the first time we vampires have had to move."

"You'll move?" said Tony, shocked.

"Do you think we're going to wait until the vault's completely blocked up?"

"Oh no!" said Tony, and gulped. "But I didn't think it would be so soon . . ."

"It won't be as soon as all that," the vampire replied, turning to the window. "And in any case, we've still got the emergency exit. Also, today's the day we hold the family council – then we'll see what happens."

"The family council? Will Anna be there too?"

"Of course."

"What about her eyes? Are they better?"

"Yes. Greg got hold of a magic potion for her."

"Really?"

"Yes. He told us he'd spent a whole night flying around, looking high and low and asking everyone – finally he came across a little old man who gave him the very last bottle of an ancient herbal remedy for all ills. It was called Devil's Tears, or something."

"He got it from a little old man, did he? Well, I never!" said Tony. "But the main thing is, it worked."

"Now I must fly," the vampire announced. "They may be needing my help."

"It's a pity I can't help at all," said Tony.

"Well, you could . . ." the vampire answered, drawing back his narrow, almost bloodless lips in a grin. His eyes ran longingly over Tony's neck.

"I – I didn't mean it like that!" stammered Tony, who suddenly found he had goose-pimples.

"Well, in that case —" said the vampire. He climbed on to the windowsill and spread out his arms under his cloak.

"Come back soon!" Tony called.

The Little Vampire did not reply. Without a word of

farewell, without even turning his head, he flew away.

Tony closed the window and undressed slowly, almost mechanically. He began to put on his pyjamas. How sorry he felt for the vampires! How miserable life was for them! Not only were they forced to live in endless darkness, but they were hounded and persecuted everywhere, too. And if they did ever find a peaceful place to stay, it was not long before someone drove them away again. They had to be frightened for their lives all the time.

Tony felt the tears run down his cheeks, but he did not wipe them away. He went over to the window and looked out into the night. Somewhere out there was the Little Vampire – perhaps in danger of his life!

Tony heard footsteps outside in the hall and his door opened.

"Are you still awake?" His mother sounded surprised, and she came into the room. "Why aren't you in bed? You haven't even drawn the curtains!" she added reproachfully.

"I couldn't sleep," Tony murmured.

"Why not?" she asked.

"There's something I had to think about," Tony answered, and he drew one hand over his eyes.

"I should think you did have something to think about!" Mum sounded exasperated. "Perhaps you were thinking about what you're going to say to the psychologist tomorrow."

Tony gave her a black look out of the corner of his eye. "Perhaps I was!" he snapped.

"But don't you try to get his goat!" Mum warned.

"His goat?" Tony snorted. "I'd rather get a vampire!" He added, in a quiet little voice, "That is, if he hasn't already flown away for ever."

"Flown away for ever?" Mum repeated in astonishment. She gave a brittle laugh. "Oh, Tony, that would be marvellous!"

"Maybe it would," said Tony through gritted teeth. "For you!"

"For all of us!" she retorted. "But you can't understand that – yet!" And with that, she left the room.

"Understand?" Tony sobbed, throwing himself down on his bed. "No, I can't understand. And I don't want to – ever!"

A Visit to the Psychologist

The next morning, still half asleep, Tony switched on his radio and just caught the last item on the news report.

". . . most unusual for this time of year. Last night, the temperature dropped to well below freezing. Black ice has made the roads hazardous. The police have asked all drivers to use public transport wherever possible."

Suddenly Tony was wide awake. Black ice, hazardous roads – it was all music to his ears! For ever since his mother once skidded her car into a tree on an icy road, she had preferred to stay home whenever frost made driving dangerous. Perhaps she would cancel the appointment with the psychologist . . .

Tony dressed himself quickly and went into the kitchen. His parents were sitting at the table, drinking coffee. The little radio on the kitchen worktop was playing music.

"Have you heard the traffic reports?" he enquired. "They say the streets are very slippery."

"Yes. I'm going to school by bus," said Mum.

Tony's heart missed a beat. "And – this afternoon?"

She laughed dryly. "Aha, you think you're going to be let off that visit to the psychologist – I see!"

"Well," said Tony with a cheeky grin, "I just didn't want you to go skidding into a tree again."

Mum gave him a deadly look. "Thank you, but we'll go by bus."

"By bus? I thought you said the psychologist lived miles away?"

"So what?" said Mum. "We'll get there somehow."

Somehow – that just about summed it up. After what seemed like an endless journey from one side of the town to the other, changing buses twice and then taking a taxi, they finally ended up outside a large, old-fashioned house. The psychologist had his consulting rooms on the ground floor. There was a brass plate beside the front door:

GEOFFREY CRUSTSCRUBBER
Marriage Guidance Counsellor
and Child Therapist

"Well, at least he's got a funny name," Tony muttered. He felt the way he did when he visited the dentist – only worse! At least with a dentist you knew what unpleasant things were in store for you, like an injection or the drill. But here, at the psychologist's . . .

"You should have brought Dad along," he remarked to his mother.

She looked pale and nervous, as if she were the one who was going to be questioned.

"Dad? Why?" she asked distractedly.

"Because it says he's a marriage guidance counsellor," he answered with a grin.

"Oh, tut," she said irritably.

Footsteps came closer, and the door was opened by a cosy-looking lady with a round face and dark hair pulled back in a bun.

"Good afternoon," she said, with such a friendly smile that for a minute Tony forgot he did not like psychologists.

"Our name's Peasbody. We have an appointment," said Mum, a little too loudly.

The lady nodded. "Please come in. My husband's expecting you."

Her husband? Tony thought, amazed and delighted. Then perhaps Mr Crustscrubber couldn't be quite as horrible as he'd expected.

Mr Crustscrubber was tall and very fat. He did not have a white coat like a doctor; instead he was wearing a pullover stretched over his stomach and a pair of baggy corduroy trousers. He had a moustache, and there were creases round his eyes as though he laughed a lot.

"Do you know why you're here?" he asked, in a nice, deep voice, studying Tony expectantly.

"Um . . ." Tony mumbled, looking over at his mother. "Didn't Mum tell you?" he tried.

Mr Crustscrubber smiled. "Of course. But I want to hear it from you."

"Mmm. Well, I . . ." Secretly, Tony had made up his mind to answer all the questions, but not to volunteer anything himself.

"Well, come on!" his mother cried impatiently. "Have you lost your tongue?"

Tony clamped his lips together furiously.

"Don't force him," said Mr Crustscrubber gently.

Exactly! Tony entirely agreed. Suddenly, he felt full of confidence, and he lifted his chin. "I think I would rather talk to Mr Crustscrubber in private," he said.

His mother gave an indignant snort and rose abruptly to her feet.

"All right then, if I'm in the way!"

"Of course you're not in the way," Mr Crustscrubber said soothingly. "But perhaps it would be helpful to talk to Tony alone to begin with."

"As you wish." Tony's mother bustled out of the room.

The Most Important Person

Tony wore a contented grin on his face as he watched his mother leave.

"That was a good idea of yours," he said, crossing his legs.

"What was?"

"Sending Mum out."

"But that was your idea."

"Yeah, well —" Tony could not help grinning. "But I didn't think you would say so too. Now she'll really be cross."

"No, I don't think she will," Mr Crustscrubber replied. "And even if she were, you're the most important person here."

A feeling of warmth and well-being filled Tony. So he was the most important person – now that *did* sound promising!

"What about Mum?" he asked. "Isn't she an important person?"

"Ah yes, your mother. Now what part does she play in all this?" Mr Crustscrubber threw the question back at Tony.

Tony made a face. "A rotten one. She's against everything that I think is fun. She's against my books,

what I like on television, and she's against my friends, too."

"She's only against a certain sort of book, isn't she?" the psychologist suggested.

"She's against my favourite ones!" Tony cried indignantly.

"What are your favourite ones?"

"*Dracula*, *Frankenstein*, anything that's creepy and exciting."

"What does your mother have against them?"

"She says they're not worth reading."

"Not worth reading?" Mr Crustscrubber repeated doubtfully. "Now, what's worth reading may be a different thing for different people."

"Exactly!" Tony nodded. "And I just love horror stories!"

"What do you like best about them?"

"They're exciting. And anyway, I believe there's something bad in everyone —" Tony broke off. He suddenly had the feeling he had said too much.

"And these books are about the bad things hidden in each of us, you mean?" said Mr Crustscrubber.

"Yes," said Tony, turning red.

"You're a young man who has observed the world around us and the people in it very closely." Mr Crustscrubber's face was serious, almost solemn. "And you think deeply about a lot of things, which is good."

Tony felt the lovely warm feeling again.

"But would you say you sometimes think *too* deeply about things?"

"What do you mean, too deeply?" Tony did not understand.

"I mean, perhaps you think too much, and don't play enough with other children."

Tony looked at him with wide-open eyes. "I don't understand."

"Your mother says you haven't got any real friends."

"No real friends?" Tony was furious. "I've got some fantastic friends!"

"She says you spend a lot of time alone in your room."

Tony's bottom lip began to jut out. "My friends haven't always got time to play. They have little jobs to do, you see."

"Little jobs?" said Mr Crustscrubber, sounding interested. "Like delivering newspapers?"

"Yes, that sort of thing," Tony answered, managing not to smile.

"I see," said Mr Crustscrubber.

There was a pause. Mr Crustscrubber rustled his note pad, then he said, "There's one other thing. Your mother says you know some vampires."

Tony tried to stay cool. "Vampires?" he repeated with deliberate calm.

"Yes." Mr Crustscrubber was looking at him carefully. "Is that true?"

"Do you believe in vampires, then?" Tony asked in return.

Mr Crustscrubber rocked his head thoughtfully this way and that. "Let's just say I'm interested in vampires." He opened a drawer and took out a thick folder. "You see, I've been developing a course of treatment for people suffering from a phobia."

"A what?"

"A phobia. That's what we call an abnormal fear of certain other people, or things. For instance, some people feel panic when they see a spider, and that's a phobia. I want to be able to help people overcome their fears through my course."

"Ah," said Tony.

"I've used it successfully with many patients. Your mother gave me the idea of trying it out on vampires."

"On vampires? Why?"

"Because they have such an overwhelming horror of daylight. If I were successful in curing them of it, it would be a sensation!"

"Would it be possible?"

Mr Crustscrubber pointed proudly to the folder. "It would be, with my course," he said.

"But . . . but I don't know any vampires," Tony replied quickly. None that would go to a psychologist, anyway, he added to himself – and that was the honest truth!

"None?" Disappointment showed on Mr Crustscrubber's chubby, red face. "But your mother —"

"Yes, Mum!" Tony cut him short. "Now, she *has* got a f- fo-"

"Phobia?" Mr Crustscrubber offered.

"Yes, exactly. It's quite weird the way she keeps bringing vampires into everything." He jumped up and ran to the door. "Ask her yourself!"

"All right, if you like," Mr Crustscrubber answered pleasantly. "Bring her in!"

Ice-Cream and Red Ears

Tony found his mother in the little waiting room at the other end of the hallway, leafing through a magazine.

"Now it's your turn!" he announced.

"Me?"

"Yes. Mr Crustscrubber wants to talk to you about your vampire phobia."

"About what?" She stared at him, shocked.

"Your abnormal fear of vampires. He's actually developed a course to help you."

Tony noticed that his mother had gone pale.

"A course – for me?" She moved to the door in confusion and disbelief.

"Good luck!" Tony called after her.

It was nearly half an hour before she came back.

"Well, how was it?" Tony asked curiously.

She only shook her head. "Let's go," she said.

On the way to the taxi rank, she suddenly asked, "Would you like an ice-cream? There's a café over there."

"An ice-cream? In this weather?" Tony was amazed. Until today, she'd always said ice-creams were something you only had in summertime.

"I feel like a cup of coffee," she said, "and if you'd like an ice-cream . . ."

"Me? Any time!" he said and grinned.

Ten minutes later a tall glass heaped with ice-cream and fruit and topped with whipped cream stood in front of Tony. At least the visit to the psychologist has been worth it for this! he thought, taking spoonfuls of ice-cream, while his mother drank her coffee in rapid little sips. When she had finished, she leaned back with a sigh.

"Mr Crustscrubber talked a lot about you," she began.

"About me?" Tony looked up from his ice-cream with an uneasy feeling, but his mother was smiling.

"Yes. He thinks there's no need for us to worry about you. You're a very alert young man, he said, and you know an amazing amount about human nature for someone of your age. You say what you think openly, and he liked that very much. If only all children were like that, he said."

Tony realized his ears were turning red.

"However, he did have one or two criticisms to make," she went on, clearing her throat.

Tony gulped. After so much praise, there had to be a disagreeable part.

"But they were of Dad and me."

"What? Dad and you?"

"Well, there were several things. The evenings we go out, for instance. Mr Crustscrubber thinks you're still too young to be left alone every Saturday night."

"Me – too young?" Tony cried indignantly.

"Yes. He suggested we should get a baby-sitter."

"A baby-sitter? For me?" That was really the end!

"Of course I don't mean literally." Mum tried to calm him. "After all, you're not a baby any more. But perhaps a nice teenager who you could play with, or who would watch television with you, or listen to tapes – whatever you felt like."

"I don't need anyone to take care of me!" said Tony furiously.

His mother smiled. "You'll certainly need to get used to the idea first."

"Used to it?" Tony cried. "You think I'm going to get used to some new scheme every couple of weeks just because it fits in with your plans? No thank you, I'm quite used to being on my own now."

His mother looked disconcerted. "Don't let's fight," she said, glancing over at two elderly ladies who were the only other customers in the café. They behaved as if they were fully occupied in dividing the large slice of gateau they had chosen, but they had clearly been listening to everything that had been said.

"We'll discuss the other things at home," said Mum quietly.

"What other things?" Tony cried angrily, not caring if anybody was listening. "It's quite enough that now I've got to have a baby-sitter!"

But Mum was obviously determined not to be provoked. "Let's just see how it goes the first time," she said soothingly. Then she asked, "Would you like something else? A piece of cake? Or a cup of hot chocolate?"

"No," Tony grunted, amazed at her sudden generosity. "I'm full up."

The journey home was no easier than the one there. Only one thing was different: his mother was going to extraordinary lengths to be nice to him. She bought him a comic at a bookstall, even though until now she had always said that such things were "trash" and only there

94

to tempt children – and their parents – to waste their money. And when Tony said he was thirsty, he was allowed – as a celebration, she explained – a can of Coca-Cola. All this seemed to have been brought about by the visit to the psychologist, and Tony certainly wasn't unhappy about that. But he still had an uneasy feeling about the "other things" she wanted to discuss with him. And about Anna and Rudolph.

As their bus drove past the cemetery, and Tony saw the high wall and the entrance gates, it hit him like an electric shock. The afternoon had been so worrying that he had hardly had time to think of the vampires and the danger that was threatening them. He wished he could get off at the next stop. He tried to get a look at the far end of the cemetery, but the tall yew trees blocked his view.

At least he was reassured by the thought that the work on the cemetery would be hit by the sudden icy weather too. If it was freezing, they couldn't dig up the earth, could they? Perhaps work on the "improvements" would now have to be put off till spring? And perhaps the vampires would be able to stay in the vault till then? Oh, that would be too good to be true!

"What are you thinking about?" asked Mum, who was sitting next to him on the bus, watching him.

"What am I thinking about?" Tony turned his gaze from the window. "I'm thinking about bed!"

Mum laughed. "I've never heard you say that before!"

"I'm exhausted!" said Tony with a yawn. "Once I'm home, I'm going straight to bed."

"The afternoon has been rather an effort," Mum agreed. "For me, too. Let's talk about the other things tomorrow."

Tony nodded in relief.

Once back home, he had a quick wash, said good

night to his parents and got into bed – with his favourite book, *Dracula*, to keep him awake.

Beating Hearts

Tony must have fallen asleep in spite of the book, because suddenly a noise startled him awake. He blinked, and recognized a small black shadow at the window.

"Rudolph!" he exclaimed.

Joyfully, he rushed over to the window and opened it.

"I think you're the one who needs eye-drops!" answered a bright voice.

"Anna!" said Tony, turning red, partly because he had mistaken her for Rudolph, and partly because he was in his baggy old pyjamas.

"May I come in?" she asked with a shy smile.

"Of course," he said, taking a step to one side. She was still looking poorly, and her appearance was not quite as neat as usual. But even with her tangled hair and crumpled cloak, he thought she was so sweet that his heart began to beat faster.

"Are your parents here?" she enquired, looking anxiously over at the door.

"Yes. I bet they're sitting in the living-room talking about me."

"About you?" Anna looked at him and smiled mischievously. "I'd like to be a fly on the wall."

"Why?"

"I'm sure they're saying nice things about you."

"I don't think so," Tony replied.

"No?" She did not believe him. "I'd only say nice things about you – nice and kind!"

Tony went red again. He wanted to change the subject, so he said, "How are your eyes?"

"They're better, thanks to Greg."

"Oh, Greg, I see," said Tony mockingly.

Anna looked at him defiantly. "You really have no right to criticize Greg! After all, was it you who managed to get hold of the Devil's Tears for me?" And before Tony could say anything, she went on, "There, you see! But Greg managed to! He spent the whole night flying around for me, asking people about Devil's Tears. And in the end —"

"— in the end he came across a little old man who gave him the very last bottle of an ancient herbal remedy – yes, yes, I know all that!" Tony interrupted.

"How do you know?"

"Rudolph told me the story."

"Story?"

"Of course it's all a story. Greg got the bottle of Tull – of Devil's Tears from me, actually." He had nearly given the game away and said Tulli-Ex.

"From you?" said Anna in amazement. She bit her lip, and Tony could almost see her thoughts churning in her head. "If that's true, then it's utterly unfair that Greg's got out of the coffin shift!"

"Of course it's true!" Tony protested, cross that she did not say a word of apology or thank him for the eye-drops. Perhaps she was too confused.

"What is the coffin shift?" he asked. "And how has Greg got out of it?"

Anna took a couple of deep breaths.

"That's why I've come," she said, "to tell you all about it." She paused. "But it's so hard," she whispered, turning away to the window.

Tony saw that her narrow little shoulders were heaving. Was she crying? He wanted to comfort her, so he said, "The frost's bound to go on. Perhaps McRookery and Sniveller will have to put off their plans for the improvements till the spring. That would be great, wouldn't it?"

"It's too late," she answered glumly.

"Why is it too late?" asked Tony, his voice trembling.

"Because the coffin shift's already begun." She turned back to Tony. Her huge eyes were glistening and wet. "You and I will never lose each other, will we?" she said softly. Then she smiled again and went over to the window.

"Wait!" Tony cried. "You must tell me what's going to happen to you all. To us!" he added with a gulp.

Anna climbed on to the windowsill. She did not look at him as she said, "We're moving to the ruins in the Vale of Doom. The family council decided yesterday. We take the first of the coffins over there tonight."

"On foot?" asked Tony.

He had once been to the Vampire Ball in the Vale of Doom, and as they were flying there, Rudolph had told him how far it was to the ruins: fifty kilometres.

"No, we fly," Anna answered. "Two vampires take a coffin between them each time, and fly with it. We call it the coffin shift."

"And all the vampires join in?"

She shook her head. "I have to look after myself, that's what my grandmother, Sabina the Sinister, said. Greg's got out of it as a reward for getting the Devil's Tears." She laughed bitterly. "I can't even prove that

he's tricked us all, otherwise I'd have to admit that the drops came from you."

"Oh no, please don't tell them that!" Tony pleaded.

"Don't worry." She smiled. Slowly she began to move her arms up and down, and immediately she started to float in the air. "All the best, Tony," she said.

"I'll see you again, won't I?" he cried in dismay.

"Yes," she said, gazing at him tenderly. "Tomorrow, if all goes well."

Then swiftly she flew away.

A Symphony in Horror

"We've got a surprise for you," Mum announced at breakfast the next morning.

"Oh?" was all Tony said. He felt he didn't need any more surprises.

"Don't you want to know what it is?" asked Dad.

"If I must . . ."

His father laughed good-naturedly. "We'd like to take you to the cinema – the six-o'clock show this evening."

"To the cinema? Tonight?" Tony was startled.

"Why not?" said Mum, as if it were a completely normal thing to do. She added mysteriously, "There's a horror film on."

"A h-horror film?" Tony stammered.

He did not want to move from his room this evening for anything, not even the most fantastic horror film in the world.

His mother picked up the newspaper from the kitchen table and read out:

" 'Nosferatu: a symphony in horror. Directed in 1922 by Friedrich Wilhelm Murnau.' Now, isn't that right up your street?"

"Yes," he murmured. His gaze fell on his school bag, which still contained his sports things from yesterday. That gave him an idea.

"I can't go to the cinema tonight," he said firmly.

"Why not?" Dad wanted to know.

"Because the Sports Gala's tomorrow," he answered, "and I want to be fit for it."

Normally he detested the word "fit", but this time he said it with relish. He knew very well how much his parents did in order to keep "fit": long walks, healthy food . . . He saw them exchange glances.

"We hadn't thought of that," said Mum.

"And now that you've become so sporty," Dad added, "the Sports Gala is definitely more important."

Tony grinned secretly.

"What's more, Mr Crustscrubber was very pleased that you're interested in sport," Mum remarked.

Tony looked up from his bowl of muesli. "Why? What's it got to do with him?" he asked resentfully.

"We were talking about your hobbies," Mum answered. "And he gave me some advice —"

"To get a baby-sitter to look after me, I know," Tony interrupted angrily.

But Mum continued calmly, "He gave me some advice, which was to do things together with you more often, things that you enjoy. That's why we wanted to take you to the cinema."

"Mr Crustscrubber would do better to mind his own business!" Tony said grumpily, but secretly he was very impressed. The psychologist seemed to have some very useful ideas.

"What else did he say?" he asked.

"He would like Dad and me to visit him together," said Mum.

Tony nearly choked. "I told you!" he said, and burst out laughing.

"What?" asked his parents together.

"Marriage guidance!" Tony giggled. "Now it's your turn!"

"Very funny!" said his father crossly.

"Yes, hilarious!" Mum agreed sourly.

"Then why aren't you laughing?" said Tony, closing his school bag with a snap.

Once outside, he was dismayed to find that it had grown warmer. Bother! he thought. Work on the cemetery will surely start again! Suddenly, Tony had the gravest doubts that all would go well with the vampires moving to the Vale of Doom. If only it were evening already . . .

The Last Time

Tony was nervous and on edge as he waited in his room for it to get dark. As soon as dusk began to fall, he pulled open the window and gazed out, but none of the vampires were to be seen. Perhaps it was still too early? Leaving the window ajar, he sat down on his bed. He switched on the light and tried to read, but he was much too worried and restless to concentrate on what was happening in the castle of Count Dracula.

From time to time, he looked over at the window. What would he do if Anna didn't come? Should he go to the cemetery by himself? After all, he still had the vampire cloak . . .

A knock on his door interrupted his thinking.

"Tony?" It was his mother's voice.

"What is it?" he asked coldly.

"I've brought you a glass of fresh orange juice," she answered, coming into the room. "I've just squeezed it. It's for tomorrow."

"For tomorrow?" Tony scoffed. "It'll be off by then!"

She laughed. "Drink it now, so that you're fit and well for the Sports Gala tomorrow."

"I'm already fit and well." He said it sullenly in order to put her off. But since the visit to the psychologist, she

105

seemed to have the patience and good nature of an angel.

"Come on, drink it up, you grumpy old bear," she said, putting the glass down on his desk. It was then that she noticed the open window.

"Why is your window open?" she exclaimed, sounding a bit more ruffled. "Do you think we put the heating on for the benefit of the birds outside?"

"For the birds?" said Tony with a grin. "Why not? Our biology teacher is always saying, 'Don't forget our feathered friends'!"

His mother gave an indignant snort and closed the window.

"Hey!" Tony protested. "Don't you know that you need fresh air when you're exercising?"

"Exercising?" she retorted hotly. "On your bed with a book? I suppose it's called gym for the eyeballs!"

Tony stifled a laugh. "Aren't I allowed a little break to catch my breath?"

He snapped the book shut and stood up. All of a sudden, he felt he could not bear this pointless sitting around. The waiting was killing him! He'd rather go to the cemetery and see for himself what was happening.

"I think I'll go and do some more training outside," he said.

"Outside?" Startled, Mum glanced out of the window. "But it's already dark."

"You didn't mind that before. And anyway, it'll be the last time."

"The last time?" She sounded doubtful.

"Sure. After all, the Sports Gala is tomorrow."

She hesitated. "All right," she said at last, and turned to go. "But don't stay out too long."

"Of course I won't."

"And don't forget to drink your orange juice."

But Tony had other things on his mind. Mum had hardly left the room before he took the vampire cloak from his cupboard, stuffed it under his jumper and ran out into the hallway. "See you later!" he called, and pulled the front door shut behind him.

Once outside, Tony did not waste any time doing silly exercises. He ran off without looking back once, and did not stop till he saw the wall of the old cemetery in front of him.

He wrapped the vampire cloak around him – just as a precaution! Then he looked round carefully, listening for any unusual noises. There was nothing suspicious, as far as he could tell, so he gritted his teeth and climbed over the wall.

The Frog Prince

Tony landed in an open space which had been stripped bare and flattened by the machines. So this is all that's left of the best bit of the cemetery, he thought, feeling angry and bitter. All the little bushes he had often hidden behind had disappeared, and so had the tall grass. He remembered how he used to wander through it, and how one day he had discovered the heart-shaped tombstones of the vampires in among it.

Now the only things spared were a couple of tall trees – and, luckily, the yew tree by the entrance to the vault. He wondered whether the tunnel would still be covered with earth, or whether McRookery and Sniveller had tracked it down and uncovered it. Or perhaps the vampires would have opened it up themselves for the coffin shift.

That was the first thing Tony had to go and find out about. He pulled the cloak over his head so that only his eyes and nose were showing, and ran over the empty space to the yew tree. There he stopped and checked the ground carefully, but there was nothing to give away the entrance to the underground vault. Tony could not see any entrance hole, nor the tunnel – just the black, churned-up earth of the cemetery.

So now the vampires were using the emergency exit over by the old chapel all the time. Tony lifted his head and looked over in the direction of the chapel. Its pointed, cone-shaped roof stood out clearly against the night sky.

Tony noticed something else too: the outlines of the two earth movers, standing by the chapel. They looked like prehistoric monsters, huge and menacing. It was just as well that they were not dangerous as long as there was no one at the steering wheel. Even so, he crept past them with an uncomfortable feeling. Somehow they seemed like the arms of McRookery and Sniveller, stretching out to get him.

But nothing happened, and Tony reached the chapel safely. He could not see the well from there yet, but that suited him fine. He pushed his back against the chapel and stood for a minute, listening. At first he could hear nothing.

Then his ears picked up a whisper. All of a sudden, he heard a muffled cry, and then a rattle.

Now Tony could not keep still any longer. He ran on tiptoe to a thick box hedge and, pushing a couple of branches to one side, looked over towards the old well.

There were three figures standing round it: two small ones and one big fat one. The two small ones were Rudolph and Anna. Tony recognized the third from her bulky shape and her wild, unkempt hair. He nearly cried out loud in horror – it was Aunt Dorothy! She had a rope in her hand, and she was tugging at it obstinately.

"Blast and damnation, it still won't budge!" Tony heard her swearing.

What wouldn't budge? Her coffin, perhaps?

"Don't get so annoyed with it, Auntie," came a bright

voice, which Tony recognized immediately. It was Anna. "Otherwise something's going to break . . ."

"Oh, fiddlesticks! I know more about moving than you do," Aunt Dorothy retorted grumpily, heaving with all her strength. Something creaked and snapped, and then there was a crash that seemed to shake the earth.

"Oh, no!" Anna's voice sounded flustered.

"The rope's broken – so what?" Aunt Dorothy said, panting. "Rudolph will just have to climb down and tie it together again!"

"Me?" Rudolph exclaimed.

"Well, who else?" Aunt Dorothy rounded on him. "You don't think I'm going to, do you?"

"No, but – Anna could!"

Tony took a deep breath. What a mean thing to do, to push his little sister forward! But this time he did not get away with it.

"You can manage," Aunt Dorothy answered with a scornful laugh. "Anna's still got to take care of herself. Or do you want her to get sand in her eyes?"

"N-no," said the Little Vampire meekly.

"Well, then! Come on, one, two, into the well with you, Frog Prince!" Aunt Dorothy commanded.

But it was not to be. For at that moment, a harsh, hacking cough could be heard from the direction of McRookery's house. It was still a long way away, but it was enough to set the vampires on red alert.

"McRookery!" Aunt Dorothy breathed, her voice full of hate. "Just let me get my claws on him! His whole garlic store won't do him any good this time."

An icy shiver ran down Tony's spine. He pulled the cloak down over his forehead.

"Wouldn't it be better to fly away?" asked Anna.

"No!" Aunt Dorothy spat. "Have you forgotten it was

that McRookery who blocked up the passage? I nearly broke my neck because of him!"

"But you can't prove that!" Anna objected.

"Hah! Who else could it have been? Besides, it's all his fault that we have to leave the vault."

"It really would be better to fly!" Anna's voice sounded urgent.

"What about my coffin? Am I supposed to leave it here in the well, plus all our family heirlooms?" Aunt Dorothy was so enraged that she was puffing loudly. "Never on my life will I do such a thing!"

The rasping cough could be heard once more, and this time it was closer.

"Don't just stand there!" Aunt Dorothy shrieked. "Do something!"

"Like what?" asked the Little Vampire.

"Distract McRookery! Off you go!"

"What will you do, Auntie?" asked Anna.

"Me? I'll climb down to my coffin and guard it." Aunt Dorothy's voice sounded almost gentle.

Tony watched as, with surprising agility, she vanished down into the well. Rudolph and Anna ran off in Tony's direction. They came to a halt only a few steps away from him, but they did not seem to have noticed him yet.

"What shall we do?" Anna whispered.

"I've had enough!" the Little Vampire grumbled. "She can jolly well manage on her own."

"What about McRookery? Who's going to distract him?"

"Aunt Dorothy can! After all, she's the one crouching in the well like the Frog Prince. Let her throw a golden ball at his head if he comes too near! In any case, it's not my coffin that's stuck!"

"You're scared!"

"Scared? I'm just being careful," said the Little Vampire.

"Anyway, why don't *you* distract him?"

"I don't trust my eyes, that's all!" Anna replied.

"You don't want to admit that you're just as frightened. Anna the Fearless – what a joke!" The vampire broke into a hoarse cackle of laughter. "Anna the Anxious would suit you better!"

That was too much for Tony. He had made up his mind not to make a sound, just to wait and see what happened. But hearing Rudolph insult Anna, he just couldn't let that pass without doing something. He slid out from his hiding place with a beating heart.

"Just leave Anna alone!" he ordered.

The Little Vampire was so startled that his mouth gaped open.

"You?" said Anna, and her pale cheeks reddened slightly.

"*I* will distract McRookery!" Tony declared, amazed at his own bravery. He suddenly felt there was nothing he would not do for Anna. "Rudolph is obviously too wet to do it!"

"Wet?" The vampire laughed scornfully. "I'm not wet – just got more brains than you!"

"Oh, Tony, would you really do it?" Anna sounded touched.

"What's more, I've already got an idea how to distract McRookery!" said Tony hastily, and before they could notice that he too was blushing, he had vanished behind the hedge.

The Cute Blond One

Tony's idea was to hide behind the earth-moving equipment. McRookery would be bound to walk past on his way to the chapel, and as soon as Tony saw him, he could run off to the exit. If all went according to plan, McRookery would chase after him and that would give the vampires time.

Now Tony could hear that rasping cough again. It sounded very near. Then he heard something else: someone swore.

"Your blasted cough! It'll spoil everything!" That was McRookery's croaky voice.

"I can't help it if I have to cough," Sniveller whined.

"You can do a lot to help it!" McRookery retorted. "You don't have to go washing your hair every single day, for a start."

"But I do!" Sniveller replied. "I've got greasy hair, you see – and dandruff!"

"Well, so have I," McRookery growled. "And I only wash my hair once a month!"

"Eeugh!" Sniveller exclaimed.

"For goodness sake, not so loud!" McRookery hissed.

"Anyway, it's your fault I've got a cough," Sniveller

whined. "You're always sending me off into the cemetery with wet hair."

"Because that's your job!" said McRookery in exasperation. "After all, you're the assistant gardener, not a hairdresser!"

"Oh, you're so horrid to me!" Sniveller complained. "What have I ever done to you?"

"Oh, do shut up!" said McRookery.

"All right then, I won't say another word," Sniveller answered, sounding hurt.

After that, it was quiet except for the sound of their footsteps. They were getting closer to the digger where Tony was hiding, quivering with excitement and waiting for the moment when they would appear.

Minutes passed – it seemed like eternity. There was nothing worse than waiting! The only sound was the gravel crunching under their feet . . . At last they appeared round the other side of the digger: the short figure of McRookery and Sniveller's tall one.

"Come on, let's see if there's anything wrong with these machines!" McRookery ordered.

"What might be wrong with them?" Sniveller was not convinced.

"Oh, kids may have been messing about round here," came the answer. "Just remember that lad we caught red-handed the other day."

"The cute blond one?"

"Cute?" McRookery spat. "He was one of those rascals whose mother and father neglect their duties as parents – it's wicked! Parents like that should be locked up, together with their badly brought-up offspring."

Tony gave an angry snort. He wouldn't be a bit sorry if that old toad McRookery did fall into Aunt Dorothy's clutches!

Unfortunately McRookery stank horribly of garlic even at ten paces or more. Tony's stomach heaved at the stinging smell.

"I thought you said we were out to hunt vampires," said Sniveller sourly.

"All in good time!" McRookery answered. "First we must check the machines. Or don't you want the driver and his mate to be able to get going again tomorrow?"

"Yeah," Sniveller growled.

"Well, then! You look at the bulldozer, I'll check the digger."

That was Tony's cue. He crept between the wheels and waited until McRookery had climbed on to the digger.

Then out Tony sprang, with a cry that was so loud and piercing it made his ears ring. At the same time, he whirled the cloak about so as to leave no doubt that he was in fact a vampire.

McRookery and Sniveller seemed to have fallen for it. They stared at him as if he were a ghost.

"A vampire!" McRookery cried, clambering down from the digger as fast as his short, fat legs would carry him.

Tony let him get within a few paces of him, then he ran off up the dark pathway, which he assumed would lead to the gate. He heard McRookery call, "Come on, we'll corner him!"

"Corner him? How?" Sniveller called back.

"Idiot!" McRookery hissed. "You run round to the right, I'll take the left!"

"You're not going to leave me on my own, are you?" Sniveller whimpered. "What if the vampire gets me?"

"For crying out loud!" McRookery swore. "Then follow me, if you're going to wet yourself!"

116

Now the path forked. Tony stopped and looked round at his pursuers.

They were panting loudly, but closing on him. He heard McRookery call out in triumph, "We've almost got him!"

But it was too soon to gloat. Tony waited till they had almost reached him, then he vanished down the path that led off to the right. It was a narrow side path and Tony did not know where it would end. He just hoped it would lead them far away from the old well. He heard McRookery give a gleeful cry of surprise.

"He's making straight for our house!' he called to Sniveller.

Tony's blood seemed to freeze in his veins. McRookery's house? That stood close to the new, white wall round the cemetery, and Tony could remember that at that point the wall was at least two metres high with no crevices or jutting stones to help him climb over it . . .

Now he felt more like a mouse in a trap than a decoy duck, until he suddenly remembered that he was wearing the vampire cloak.

Tony ran faster to increase his lead. Then he spread out his arms under the cloak and, with mounting excitement, he felt his feet lift off the ground. He made a couple of powerful arm movements and he was flying.

A feeling of enormous relief ran right through his body. McRookery and Sniveller could run as fast as a fire-engine – they'd never catch him now! He flew up over the white wall and away to the playground next to his block of flats. There, he landed behind a bush and took off the cloak.

Suddenly someone tapped him on the back. Tony whipped round in fright – and found himself looking straight into Anna's face.

The Pledge

A change seemed to have come over her. The look she gave him was serious and thoughtful, and she did not smile.

"Did something go wrong?" Tony asked anxiously.

"No. Rudolph and Aunt Dorothy are now on their way to the Vale of Doom – and I must follow them," she added gently. "I've just got to check the vault to make sure we haven't forgotten anything."

Then Tony knew what was the matter. He felt a lump in his throat. Was this farewell for ever?

"You really helped us back there," she said softly. "Thank you."

"Oh, I enjoyed it," he said casually.

She gave him a look that was full of tenderness. "Won't you come with us?"

"With you?" Tony shrank away in surprise. "No!"

Anna's shoulders sagged. "You should never make a wish," she said in a voice that Tony could barely hear. "Then you won't ever be disappointed."

"Anna!"

She stood there looking so sad and lost that Tony was sorry he had been uncaring and unkind.

"I didn't mean to hurt you, I promise. I . . . you see, I

just don't want to become a vampire, that's all. But I still like you," he added, in embarrassment.

"I like you, too!" said Anna, and now, as she looked at him, the sadness had gone from her eyes. "And we'll see each other again – soon!"

She gave a smile that lit up her little face from inside, and pointed to the vampire cloak, which Tony still had in his hand.

"You can keep that," she declared in a firmer voice, "as a pledge that we won't lose each other." Then she turned away and, before Tony could say anything, the darkness had swallowed her up.

As a pledge . . . Tony's fingers slid over the rough material, with its many holes and tears, almost as if it were a religious object. Suddenly, the cloak took on a whole new meaning for him. It wasn't just any old vampire cloak; it was a part of Anna, and a part of Rudolph, too, of course.

With a sigh, Tony thought of the two vampires and their coffin shift. He hoped it had all gone smoothly. Very carefully, as if it were something fragile and priceless, he folded up the cloak and hid it under his jumper. As he did so, he was quite amazed that he wasn't upset by its mouldy smell any more. On the contrary, now it reminded him of Anna and Rudolph. Tonight he would put the cloak under his pillow.

Slowly, deep in thought, Tony made his way home. Suddenly everything seemed so unreal: the brightly lit stairway, the lift, even his own front door.

Tony took a deep breath, and pressed the doorbell.

Follow the spine-tingling adventures of Tony and his vampire friends in the next book in this chilling series:

The Little Vampire in the Vale of Doom